Silver Meadows Summer

ALSO BY EMMA OTHEGUY

Martí's Song for Freedom

Pope Francis: Builder of Bridges

Silver Meadows Summer

Emma Otheguy

Alfred A. Knopf · New York

Text copyright © 2019 by Emma Otheguy
Jacket art and interior illustrations copyright © 2019 by Kailey Whitman

All rights reserved. Published in the United States by Alfred A. Knopf,
an imprint of Random House Children's Books,
a division of Penguin Random House LLC, New York.

Knopf, Borzoi Books, and the colophon are registered trademarks
of Penguin Random House LLC.

Grateful acknowledgment is made to Henry Holt and Company and to Jonathan Cape,
an imprint of the Random House Group Limited, London, for permission to reprint
an excerpt from "In Time of Cloudburst" by Robert Frost, from *The Poetry of Robert Frost,*
edited by Edward Connery Lathem. Copyright © 1969 by Henry Holt and Company.
Copyright © 1936 by Robert Frost. Copyright © 1964 by Lesley Frost Ballantine.
Used by permission of Henry Holt and Company and Jonathan Cape,
an imprint of the Random House Group Limited. All rights reserved.

Visit us on the Web! rhcbooks.com

Educators and librarians, for a variety of teaching tools, visit us at RHTeachersLibrarians.com

Library of Congress Cataloging-in-Publication Data
Names: Otheguy, Emma, author.
Title: Silver Meadows summer / Emma Otheguy.
Description: First edition. | New York : Alfred A. Knopf, 2019. |
Summary: "Eleven-year-old Carolina moves with her family from Puerto Rico
to upstate New York, where she attends Silver Meadows camp with her cousin,
finds an abandoned cottage, and reclaims parts of the life she left in
Puerto Rico." —Provided by publisher
Identifiers: LCCN 2018018399 | ISBN 978-1-5247-7323-6 (hardcover) |
ISBN 978-1-5247-7324-3 (hardcover library binding) | ISBN 978-1-5247-7326-7 (ebook)
Subjects: | CYAC: Moving, Household—Fiction. | Family life—New York
(State)—Fiction. | Artists—Fiction. | Cousins—Fiction. |
Farms—Fiction. | Camps—Fiction. | Puerto Ricans—New York
(State)—Fiction. | New York (State)—Fiction.
Classification: LCC PZ7.1.O87 Sil 2019 | DDC [Fic]—dc23

The text of this book is set in 12-point Bembo.
Interior design by Trish Parcell

Printed in the United States of America
April 2019
10 9 8 7 6 5 4 3 2 1

First Edition

Para mis primos veraniegos,
y en particular
Daniel, Amaya, Alina, Arabella y Hugh

Part One

¡Qué descansada vida
la del que huye el mundanal ruïdo,
y sigue la escondida
senda por donde han ido
los pocos sabios que en el mundo han sido!

What a peaceful life!
To flee the hustle-bustle
and follow the hidden path
down which have traveled
the few wise men—who in this world have been!

—Fray Luis de León (1527–1591),
    "Vida retirada"

Chapter One

Carolina wondered why none of the adults had noticed how uncomfortable it was to stand around on this shadeless lawn. The sun poured down everywhere but under the big oak tree, where Carolina's little brother, Daniel, was playing. She left the adults talking and squatted next to him.

"Look, Carolina," Daniel said. "It's like silver." He skimmed his hand over the grass, scattering water droplets.

The grass was smooth and silky, and robed in a glistening layer of dew. "Liquid silver," Carolina said. She liked the grass here in upstate New York; how it was thin and slippery, not hard like the grass at home. But even at the thought, Carolina felt a twinge in her heart. Guiltily, she spread her fingers and patted the top of the grass, letting the stalks tickle her lightly, willing herself to remember: short grass, wide stalks, and scratchy.

"I'm going to make a silver braid," Daniel said, but his ripping and twisting wiped away the dew, and the blades of grass turned green and shiny in his hands.

Carolina found a twig and broke it into small pieces. "If you make another braid, we can build a bridge." Gently, she pushed the little sticks into the ground, and balanced Daniel's tiny braid on top of two of them.

"It'll be for fairies," Daniel said excitedly, ripping out three fresh pieces of grass, "with teeny-tiny feet."

"We have to make boards for the bridge, otherwise it'll be like a tightrope." Carolina hunted for loose scraps of bark, sifting through the rocks and dirt at the foot of the tree for something that could be a board. She found a dry, rough chip of tree bark and wriggled onto her stomach to add it to the tiny bridge. As she grabbed for more grass to use as decoration, she felt a familiar rush, like all her blood was speeding to her fingers, to steady her hands and focus her mind. It was how she always felt when she started a new art project. Señora Rivón said that Carolina needed to relax, not to force her artwork so much, but Señora Rivón wasn't here now, and anyway, Carolina wasn't painting. It was wonderful, to be imagining with Daniel, to have her fingers moving again, twisting grass and making something tiny and magical. As soon as she got a minute alone, Carolina would draw a fairy on a bridge. Daniel would like that. Carolina rubbed the bark, trying to memorize the texture so she could draw it later.

She was so lost in their project that for a while she forgot everything. She forgot about the Realtor sign, and her boarded-up house in Puerto Rico, and her special spot that would now **belong to** someone else. Then a car door slammed shut, and Mami appeared, casting a long shadow over the lawn. She was carrying a suitcase in one hand.

"Can you two help Papi with the bags? He's carrying a lot."

Daniel ran ahead toward the car while Carolina scrambled to her feet. Mami put an arm around her. "What were you doing with Dani?" Mami asked as they walked to the car.

"Oh, you know," Carolina said. "I was helping him make something with the grass. When I have time I'm going to draw him a fairy bridge." She pulled the last suitcase from the trunk of the car and walked with Mami toward Tía Cuca and Uncle Porter's house. "If we were at home I could paint it for him, at Señora Rivón's."

Mami sighed. "Mi amor, I know you miss Señora Rivón, but aren't you a little old for this stuff? All these fairies and painting—it's okay for Dani, but now that you're eleven you need to keep your feet on the ground and help Mami and Papi, okay?"

It was one thing about the fairies, Carolina thought, but painting—Mami was the one who had noticed Carolina drawing and taken her to Señora Rivón four years ago. She'd sat with Carolina in Señora Rivón's studio and sipped a soft drink while Señora Rivón told Carolina about learning to paint. Carolina remembered condensation gathering on the red soda can and dripping onto Mami's red-painted fingernails. Mami complained later that she would melt in that sunny studio, but every Tuesday since then, she had driven Carolina to her lessons, and never once waited in the car. Mami was the one who always came inside to see Carolina's progress.

"Okay, Caro?" Mami said, calling her by her nickname.

Carolina nodded but said nothing. She and Mami were the last ones in the house, and Uncle Porter shut the door behind them. The door had rubber strips around it, so when you opened it there was a sound like a plunger, and when you closed it, a *whoosh*. Carolina waited for Uncle Porter to turn the lock, but he didn't. She frowned. Their house in Puerto Rico had a locking iron gate in front of a door that also locked. They had kept the windows open for the breeze, but the door they locked. Then again, locked or unlocked, once Uncle Porter pulled the door shut, this house seemed completely sealed.

Tía Cuca put down Daniel's bag next to the staircase. "Do you want the tour now?"

"Oooh! Yes!" Mami gushed.

Carolina shivered and rubbed her arms. Goose bumps prickled her skin.

Uncle Porter must have seen Carolina shivering, because he stopped and cocked his head to the side. "Are you cold?" He glanced at the thermostat on the wall, and Carolina could see his bald spot. "It's probably silly for us to keep it this cool. But it's our first house with central air. Once the summer really gets going, you'll be happy for it, trust me."

Carolina nodded, trying to smile. She hadn't seen Uncle Porter in three years, and she had been only eight then. She didn't remember talking to him on that trip—he had just seemed like another piece of Tía Cuca.

Mami put a hand on Carolina's shoulder. "She's fine, Porter. Aren't you, Carolina?" There was a tightness to Mami's grip on her shoulder that made Carolina smile even wider, that made her clear her throat and find her voice.

"Yes—I'm great."

Mami went ahead into the kitchen, but Papi hung behind. "Why don't you go get a sweater from your suitcase?" he suggested quietly.

Carolina nodded gratefully and slipped back to the entry. She laid her suitcase flat and unzipped it. A smell of home, of fresh linens, of violets layered over dampness, rose from inside. Afraid the scent would escape into this scentless house, Carolina grabbed a sweater and quickly shut the suitcase and rolled it into a corner. The suitcases seemed all wrong in this sparse entry. Carolina loved for things to be neat and orderly, but there was something unnatural about the cleanness of this house. On the drive from the airport, Uncle Porter had told her the house had just been built and even the street was new. A year ago, this area had been a tangle of dirt back roads. Still, Carolina wondered whether the air-conditioning sucked away dust and clutter, leaving behind a house that would forever feel vast and hollow.

Carolina counted forks out of a kitchen drawer. "Should I set a place for Gabriela?" Carolina was trying to be helpful, even though she didn't know where anything went, and there were so many drawers and cabinets in this kitchen that she kept having to ask.

"Of course! She'll be home soon!" Tía Cuca always talked in exclamations, as if everything Carolina said was just delightful. "She's excited to see you; it's just that since we moved to this house she's been over at her friend Alyssa's constantly. We've never been walking distance from her friends before!"

"I'm excited to see her too," Carolina said, but her words got lost in Mami's enthusiastic shouts from the other side of the kitchen.

"I can't believe it's been three years! Caro, it'll be perfect—you'll get to meet all of Gabriela's friends!" To Tía Cuca, Mami said, "Caro's never had many friends; she keeps to herself too much."

Caro fumbled with the spoons, wishing Mami wouldn't talk about her like that, as if she weren't there at all.

"I don't understand," Mami went on. "When I was her age, all I wanted to do was be with other kids, but Caro is always alone."

"Ay, no te preocupes tanto," Tía Cuca interjected. *Don't worry so much.* It was true that Caro hadn't been close to the kids at her school, but she didn't see what was wrong with that. She'd had artwork and Daniel to keep her company. She had never been lonely.

She grabbed another place setting from the drawer and left Mami and Tía Cuca to it. She set the table in the kitchen. There, sliding glass doors led to a deck overlooking the yard. Uncle Porter had suggested they eat out on the deck, but Tía Cuca had complained that there were too many bugs. Carolina couldn't quite believe Tía Cuca was afraid of bugs: Mami certainly wasn't. Sometimes Tía Cuca and Mami seemed so similar that they blended together, their loud and happy voices talking at once, their wide and toothy smiles matching perfectly. But other times Carolina couldn't believe they were sisters, that Tía Cuca, too, had grown up in Puerto Rico, and not in some sealed-off house in upstate New York.

"Hey, everyone."

Carolina looked up, and they all stopped what they were doing.

Gabriela stood in the entry with a tote bag slung over one shoulder. She pulled out her earbuds and strode across the room to give Mami and Papi a hug. She waved at Tía Cuca and Uncle Porter as if they were strangers in the park and not her parents, then hugged Carolina awkwardly.

Gabriela was *longer* than Carolina remembered. She had long legs, and long black hair. She wore dangly earrings, and a neon-green *Is It Friday Yet?* T-shirt. The braces she'd worn were gone, and now Gabriela had a smile as big as Tía Cuca's.

Mami couldn't wait to talk to Gabriela. "Your mom told me you love living closer to your friends!"

"It is nice. Our old house was all the way out in the country. Plus now we have all this space." Gabriela grinned.

Mami laughed. "Which you barely got to enjoy before

we showed up to crowd you." Mami reached into her purse. "Here, we brought you a little something."

"Ana, you shouldn't have!" Tía Cuca called from the counter, where she was loading chicken onto a platter.

"It's really nothing," Mami said.

"Thank you," said Gabriela as she tore the pink-and-black wrapping off the package, letting the paper fall to the floor. Tía Cuca, on her way to the table with the chicken, snatched up the paper in a flash and tossed it in the recycling.

"A Chiquifancy cell phone case! Neat!" Gabriela was already popping the old glitter case off her phone and replacing it with the one Mami had brought her.

"I heard you were a fanatic, Gabs, and that you had your own phone, so it made sense."

Gabriela stuck her phone back in her pocket, letting her earbuds dangle over her shoulders. "Yeah, I've had a phone for two years. Time for an upgrade, *right, Daddy*?" Gabriela winked dramatically at Uncle Porter.

Carolina waited for Mami's famous lecture, the one Mami had practiced on Caro and Dani every year before school started, about how no kid should need their own phone before high school. At Carolina's old school in Puerto Rico, where Mami had been a seventh-grade teacher until just a few weeks ago, that speech was famous. Mami had slides and statistics to back it up and everything.

But instead of launching into her preprogrammed lecture, Mami smiled brightly.

Carolina stared at Mami, wondering if she was listening

to herself, if she knew what she was saying, or if she was just that determined to be chipper. More importantly, Carolina wanted to know when Mami had started calling Gabriela *Gabs*. They'd been in New York for only a couple of hours.

Gabriela popped her earbuds back in her ears and helped set the table, singing Chiquifancy lyrics under her breath and wiggling her hips as she rummaged for napkins.

Chiquifancy was so popular you couldn't walk down the street without someone singing *Canta, y baila, y cha-cha conmigo* and dancing the Fancy, Chiqui's signature dance. Mami said they should be proud that a Puerto Rican was so popular, but privately Carolina had hoped that kids in New York would be less into the Fancy, which always made her feel clumsy and slow. No such luck. Chiquifancy was officially *everywhere*.

Uncle Porter sidled up next to Gabriela, pretending to dance, but with so little rhythm that Carolina laughed out loud. He plucked Gabriela's earbud out of her ear. "Dinnertime!"

Tía Cuca insisted on serving everyone, even though Mami protested that even Daniel was perfectly capable of passing things around. When everyone was eating, Tía Cuca launched into camp talk. "Gabriela, you should introduce Carolina to Alyssa and Jamie tomorrow, okay?"

Carolina swirled her lettuce around in a puddle of dressing. She could tell from Gabriela's quick up-and-down scan that her cousin was sizing her up, and suddenly, her old school's uniform polo seemed childish. Carolina wanted to blurt out that she didn't usually wear uniform stuff in the summer, that all their other clothing had been packed, but she kept her mouth shut.

Gabriela flipped her shiny hair over her shoulder. "Yeah. I'll introduce you to Alyssa and Jamie."

Uncle Porter grabbed Gabriela's hand and said teasingly, "So you and Alyssa painted your nails pink to get ready for farm camp? I'm sure the cows will appreciate your style."

Gabriela rolled her eyes. "Daddy, Alyssa and I are too old to do farm stuff at camp anyway. Lydia lets us just hang out and talk. We'll be the oldest campers this year, remember?"

Uncle Porter clapped his hand to his heart in mock surprise. "Do you mean to tell me that you're *thirteen*? I think I almost forgot for five minutes!"

"Thirteen!" Tía Cuca wailed. "I still can't believe it."

"It's not like it's news," Gabriela said. "My birthday was four months ago."

"Still." Tía Cuca shook her head. "I just can't believe that next summer we won't have a reason to visit Silver Meadows every day."

Mami was twisting the small hairs at the back of her neck, holding her head at an angle. "Maybe Carolina and Dani will go again next year."

Carolina was almost glad to see Mami so uncertain—not that she liked seeing Mami nervous, but in it Carolina saw a glimmer of hope: maybe they wouldn't stay. Mami and Papi kept telling her it was permanent, that Papi would find a job and they would get their own house in New York. But then, there was that kernel of uncertainty in Mami's tone: *maybe* Carolina and Dani would go to Gabriela's camp next summer. Or maybe they'd be back in Puerto Rico, back at home where they belonged.

Uncle Porter started clearing the table. "I just hope Lydia is still up for running this whole operation next summer."

"Why wouldn't she be?" Gabriela asked.

"It's a lot of work to keep up a farm," Uncle Porter said.

"Oh, but it's so nice!" Tía Cuca said. She turned to Carolina and Dani. "You kids will love it. Lydia treats all the kids like her own family."

"I've never been on a farm before." Carolina tucked her hair behind her ear.

"Lydia will make you feel right at home. The farm isn't far from our old place; we used to visit all year round, and I can tell you that Lydia is just the sweetest."

"What kind of animals does she have?" Daniel chirped. "I like chickens, but I'm not petting any pigs." He held a finger out at Tía Cuca. "I mean it. No pigs."

Everyone laughed, including Tía Cuca.

"Dani, how do you even know you like chickens?" Carolina asked.

"I just do," Dani said. "They go *co-co-co*!"

"It's *bok-bok-bok* in English," Mami corrected him, and Dani took off into the other room, flapping his arms and clucking all the way.

"She mostly has cows," Uncle Porter said to the air.

"I don't get it," Carolina said. Her ears turned hot as

{13}

everyone put down the plates and platters they were carrying to listen. "Umm—" she stammered, wishing she hadn't said anything. "You don't even like bugs, Tía Cuca. But you like farms?"

For some reason, everyone thought this was hysterically funny, and Caro stood shifting her weight from one foot to the other until Tía Cuca answered. "I'm not much of an outdoors person, you're right. And Lydia does like to get you kids out and about on the farm—"

"She'll have you muck out the barn and everything," Uncle Porter added.

"But I love Lydia and I love that there's a camp right in Larksville because of her—the only other camp is three towns over," Tía Cuca went on.

"Besides, the fresh air is good for you," Uncle Porter added.

"I'm sure Caro will have a great time," Mami concluded. "Especially since she'll be with Gabriela. We're very grateful to all of you."

Carolina tried to make her face look grateful, and not nervous. She noticed Papi smiling at her, but before she could smile back he dropped his gaze to his hands, so that Carolina smiled only to his hair, thick and black.

As they made their way upstairs after dinner, Tía Cuca slipped her arm around Carolina's waist. "Let me show you the room we chose for you."

Except she said *show* like *choe,* and Gabriela groaned from behind them. "Ma, it's *show. Shhhh.* Got it?"

Mami shook her head. "I do that, too, Cuca, even though I'm an English teacher!"

Tía Cuca laughed, and squeezed Carolina a little tighter, so that Carolina's face touched her aunt's hair. It smelled flowery, with a hint of that metallic scent from hair dryers, and Carolina was relieved when Tía Cuca let her go and turned the knob to a door in the corner. "This is your room, Caro!"

Carolina must have jumped away from Tía Cuca too quickly, because Mami frowned. *Gracias?* she mouthed from behind Cuca.

"Oh—yeah," Carolina said. "I mean, umm—"

Gabriela's eyes shot up, and Carolina cringed, realizing how awkward she sounded. She paused for a minute, then took a deep breath. "Thank you, Tía Cuca. It's wonderful."

It had taken her a minute to find the words in English. It wasn't that it was *hard* to speak English, she spoke it okay, but here it was relentless. It made her tired. She realized that since Gabriela had gotten home, the only words she'd heard in Spanish were Chiquifancy lyrics. Uncle Porter and Gabriela didn't speak Spanish, and around them her family's normal back-and-forth between Spanish and English evaporated.

Alone in the room, Carolina sighed and pulled her sketchbook out of her backpack. She laid it flat on the bare desk, and looked around for a cup or a mug to keep her pencils, but couldn't find anything. The room was tidy, and the furniture was sparse: a nightstand with a lamp, a bed with a sky-blue comforter. She sat down and spaced her pencils out around the desk, just to fill the empty space.

She made some light lines on the page, envisioning the fairy bridge she'd wanted to draw for Daniel. After a few minutes, she tossed her pencil down on the paper and crossed her arms.

The paper felt so small, the pencil strokes too light and stiff. At Señora Rivón's, the easels had held canvases, big ones, large enough that Carolina had moved her whole arm, her whole body even, with every brushstroke. She remembered the wet paint, how it glided, how it felt like dancing, sliding the color this way and that.

Sternly, Carolina told herself to make do, and pushed the memory out of her mind. She picked up the pencil and drew Daniel's bridge.

Papi poked his head in. "Qué descansada vida," he remarked, and kissed her good night. Papi was like that, always quoting poetry. Every time he saw Carolina drawing, he'd say *Qué descansada vida—What a peaceful life*. It was from a poem about fleeing the hustle and bustle, and following a hidden, secret path. Papi thought it described Carolina perfectly, and maybe it did. After Papi closed the door, she drew an opening in the trees beyond Daniel's fairy bridge, a secret path all her own.

"Caro?"

Carolina dropped her pencil in surprise. "Dani! Aren't you supposed to be in bed?"

"Um, it's a little too quiet in my room. I thought it would be better in here. But it's not."

"I know what you mean." Their house in Puerto Rico had been open and airy, with overhead fans and a breeze from the patio to cool them off, and carry in the noises from outdoors: the traffic from the main road, just past the gate that separated their little community from the rest of San Juan, and the coquís, the tiny brown frogs that lived in their yard and sang all night long.

Their house was locked up now, and the gate around the front yard and the terraza, the porch in the back, had been padlocked shut. Mami and Papi were going to sell the house: before they left, Mami's cousin Conchita had buried a statue of Saint Joseph upside down in the ground. She'd told Mami it would help the house sell quickly.

Carolina shivered. Daniel was right: it was quiet, so quiet here. Just the constant sound of the central air, and nothing else. She picked up Daniel and carried him to his room, where she tucked him in tight.

"Close your eyes and pretend you're on the terraza at home," she told him.

Daniel popped open one eye. "Maybe you could draw me a picture. So I don't forget?"

"Tomorrow," Carolina promised. "Now imagine the tiles, the blue-and-white ones. Imagine the wind chimes jingling, and birds swooping through. The goldfish are swimming in the little fountain, splashing the virgencita."

Daniel's body relaxed. It had been his job to feed the goldfish that swam around the statue of Mary.

"Now imagine it's night. All the birds have flown away, and Papi turned off the lights. *Co-quí.*" Carolina imitated the sound of the little brown frogs, repeating the two syllables they made again and again: *"Co-quí, co-quí."*

Even after Daniel fell asleep, Carolina kept repeating that sound, until she ran out of voice, and the rattling of the air around them filled her ears.

Chapter Two

The farther they got from Tía Cuca and Uncle Porter's house, the older the world became. They drove through Larksville's downtown, which was really only one intersection, and Carolina liked the sturdy brick post office and the tiny steepled church with its worn wooden doors. There were a few more houses after the church, but then the houses ended abruptly, and they were truly in the countryside. There were pastures on each side of the road, interrupted only by gray silos and the dusty clapboard of a stray barn.

It was hilly here, Carolina realized. You couldn't tell from Uncle Porter and Tía Cuca's perfectly leveled, brand-new street, but in the farmland the pastures rolled and wrinkled into the distance, with patches of light grass and patches of dark. They seemed to move, and watching them reminded Carolina of being in a boat, cruising in the Caribbean sun:

these hills, tumbling in every direction around her, were like the sea had always been for Carolina, chaotic and nerve-racking when she looked too closely, but from a distance, peaceful and green, all the colors blending together into one complete sea, one complete countryside.

The car climbed a large hill, forcing Carolina to lean back in her seat. When they reached the top, a farm spanned the valley before them. Carolina could see swaths of grass and fences, and rows of crops growing. They rolled down the hill and pulled up in front of a sign swinging from a lamppost. WELCOME TO SILVER MEADOWS.

"Have a good day!" Tía Cuca called as Gabriela, Carolina, and Daniel climbed out of the car.

Mami got up from the passenger seat and closed the door behind her. Ahead of them, Gabriela checked her phone, savoring her last few minutes before camp started. Caro watched her stop beneath the lamppost, her long hair swinging in front of her face, the new Chiquifancy cell phone case glinting in the sunlight.

Caro and Dani lingered by the car with Mami.

"I'll miss you," Caro said impulsively, and Mami pulled her in for a hug.

"It's just a few hours." Mami patted Caro's hair.

"I know, but—" Caro hesitated. She felt teensy tiny and clumsily big all at once. She wanted to hear Mami call her Carolinita, *my little Caro,* like she'd done when Caro was younger, but just the thought seemed childish.

Not seeing Caro's face, Mami pulled away. "Okay, you two, be good. Caro, keep an eye on Dani."

"I'm always good." Dani batted his eyelashes dramatically, and Mami and Caro both shook their heads.

"I mean it," Mami said. "Uncle Porter and Tía Cuca had to pull some strings to get you scholarships for this camp. It was *very* nice of Lydia to have you. Do you understand?"

Caro and Dani nodded.

"And, Caro, try and make a good impression on Gabriela and her group, okay? None of your antisocial stuff this time. Make a fresh start of things here."

Caro didn't say anything at all. She wasn't antisocial, and for a moment she hated Mami for deciding to bring her here, for wanting so desperately for Caro to have friends, the kind of popular friends who listened to Chiquifancy and never talked about fairy bridges made of grass. Carolina could taste failure, the disappointment Mami would feel if no one at camp liked her.

Then Mami got back into the car and Tía Cuca waved again before they drove away. The flash of anger passed, and Carolina felt again too small in a too-large self. She gripped Daniel's hand tightly as they went to meet Gabriela by the lamppost.

Gabriela slid her phone into her back pocket. Chiquifancy's wide smile peeked out from inside. "Lydia doesn't let us have these out at camp. Come on, I'll show you around."

They followed Gabriela through the parking lot and past a one-story building. Behind the yellow building and its white trim, fields stretched out and melted into pastures, and past the pastures, a green hill loomed over the farm.

"That building's the camp center, but everyone always

waits around on the playground. We're early." Gabriela motioned for them to follow her to the back of the building.

"Look, Caro," Daniel whispered as they passed a patch of grass. "Silver."

Carolina squeezed his hand. "Liquid silver," she whispered back. It was a relief to be away from the new house, out amidst this grassy world, where it was still dewy but getting warmer every minute.

The playground buzzed with kids, talking or texting or hitting a tetherball back and forth. Gabriela spotted her friends and waved frantically. "Alyssa! Hey! I'm here!"

Carolina squinted at the tiny blond girl hurrying toward them. Her first thought was that this couldn't possibly be Gabriela's friend Alyssa. She just didn't look old enough—shorter than Carolina, with her hair half-up, half-down and clipped in place with a pink barrette. But as she came closer Carolina noticed that her teeth were perfect and straight like Gabriela's, and that in spite of her small size the shape and lines of her face were those of a teenager. Her chipper voice carried far as she shouted hello.

"Hi, Alyssa! Hi, Jamie!" Gabriela called back.

Carolina hadn't even noticed Jamie. She was as tall as Gabriela, but she slouched, and she trailed behind Alyssa, so Carolina wouldn't have known they were together if Gabriela hadn't said hello.

"Is this your cousin?" Alyssa chirped.

Daniel tugged on Carolina's sleeve. "Can I go play tetherball? Everyone keeps getting it wound around the pole."

She nodded, but it was like being torn apart, or left at sea. She hadn't been separated from Daniel for so much as an hour since they left Puerto Rico—even before they left, ever since the school year had ended a few days ago, and they'd been at home helping Mami pack.

"Yeah, this is my cousin Carolina," Gabriela said offhandedly. Carolina tried to stand straight and alert.

"What was that?" Jamie asked, not unkindly.

Before Carolina could answer, Gabriela cut in, "It's Caro-*leena*. Like Nina. Or Tina."

Alyssa hoisted a sequined beach bag higher on her shoulder. "You're going to be in our camp group. Lydia always picks the groups by age and there aren't enough thirteen-year-olds to make a group, so we have all the elevens and twelves too."

Carolina nodded. Petite or not, Alyssa was clearly in charge.

"This is Jamie," Alyssa said, even though it was obvious.

Jamie gave her a little nod. "Was that your little brother?"

Alyssa rolled her eyes. "Jamie's like the mother's helper extraordinaire of the whole town. She loves little kids."

Jamie shrugged. "He seemed sweet."

Gabriela pulled a magazine out of her tote bag and settled down on the ground. "Come on, I already took all the quizzes, but you-all haven't."

"Hiya!" A girl with a long braid and booming voice interrupted them. "I just asked Lydia, and I'm going to be in your group this summer."

Alyssa sighed. "That's great, Jennifer."

Jennifer turned to Carolina. "Hi, have we met?"

Gabriela cut in. "That's my cousin Carolina. She just moved here."

"What part of Larksville? I know all the old houses. But not all the new ones," Jennifer added, with a glance at Alyssa.

Before Carolina could speak, Gabriela jumped in again. "Her family's staying with us for a while. Just until her dad finds another job. They just—they just moved and all." Gabriela bent her head back to her magazine, but Carolina caught her looking sideways at Alyssa. Apparently she'd left out that detail before.

"Jennifer, knock off the third degree. We're looking at a magazine," Alyssa said.

Jennifer shrugged, put her hands in her pockets, and looked up at the sky. She whistled, as if the clouds were the most interesting thing in the world.

Gabriela moved the magazine closer to Carolina, and she understood without words that she was supposed to ignore Jennifer and get interested in the magazine. But Carolina couldn't stop staring, not for the life of her. Jennifer's braid stretched all the way to her butt, and there was something *in* it. A paintbrush was stuck into it, so that the bristles popped out halfway up the braid. Jennifer's backpack was bulging, even though Carolina knew from double-checking and triple-checking the camp mailings that all they were supposed to bring were swim clothes and a towel. To top everything off, Jennifer's overalls were splattered with paint.

"Are you—?" Carolina ignored Gabriela's warning look. "Are you a painter?"

Jennifer stopped whistling and grinned at Carolina. She had three different-colored rubber bands on her braces: red, yellow, and green. Carolina hadn't known it was even *possible* to get more than one color. "My dad's a painter. I help him sometimes. But mostly I like to make things that you can hold in your hands. Painting is just too flat, don't you think?"

Carolina didn't know how to respond. Señora Rivón had taught her all about perspective, about how to bring dimension into painting, and she didn't think it was flat, not at all. But if Jennifer's dad was a painter, maybe he knew . . . except—Carolina's heart beat quickly—what kind of painter was her dad? Maybe he painted houses, but maybe he painted canvases, too, landscapes of rolling pastures like the ones all around here, the ones Carolina longed to paint.

A bell clanged, and Gabriela shoved the magazine in her bag. "Come on, Carolina, we have to go inside. Camp is starting."

Gabriela and Caro trailed into the yellow one-story building behind the other kids, just ahead of Alyssa and Jamie.

"Morning, Sam! Morning, Lisa!" A woman with short gray hair stood in the doorway, high-fiving each kid as they entered. "Hey, Gabs," the woman said, and gave Gabriela a one-armed hug as they came through the doorway.

"Hi, Lydia," Gabriela said. "This is my cousin Carolina."

"Pleased to meet you." Lydia stuck out her hand, and they shook. "I've already made the acquaintance of your brother." She jerked her thumb toward the inside of the building, where there were two big round tables. Daniel was standing on a chair with a kid with big ears and curly hair, locked in an intense staring contest.

"You blinked! I saw you blink!" the curly-haired kid yelled.

"That's Ben," Lydia said. "I smell double trouble this summer."

"I'll go tell him to get down," Carolina said quickly.

"No need." Lydia smiled. "Those chairs have seen worse, I promise you." She waved Caro and Gabriela along and ushered Alyssa and Jamie inside behind them.

Gabriela showed Carolina a long row of hooks, just past the entrance, where they left their totes and backpacks. "We're at the other table," she said, leading Caro past Daniel and Ben's table, to the other side of the room, near a window that looked onto a parking lot with a tractor, and a greenhouse just past the parking lot. Just as Alyssa had predicted, Gabriela, Alyssa, Jamie, Carolina, and Jennifer were all at the same table.

Gabriela kept whispering information to Carolina while everyone else settled down. "The little kids sit at the other table and we sit here. We're all girls because Ryan Johnson went to his uncle's for the summer and Sebastian goes to sleepaway camp."

"The other group's bigger," Caro noticed as a teenager with a whistle around her neck pulled Ben off the chair. She told him to sit, then came over to the older kids' table.

"Hi! You must be Carolina," she said. "I just met your little brother. I'm Yuan, and I'm going to be the counselor for your group."

"Yuan was our counselor last year," Gabriela explained.

"That's Josh, he's the counselor for the younger kids." Yuan pointed to a teenager with a short beard and the same whistle as Yuan's around his neck. "Hey, Josh! New camper!"

Carolina waved just as Lydia clapped her hands. Everyone turned their attention to the back of the room, where there was a small kitchen and a door to a cubicle office. Lydia stood in front of a window just next to the office door. The window looked out onto the playground and the fields and hill behind it.

"Kids, it's so good to have you back," Lydia said earnestly. "We're going to have a great time this summer." She pointed to an easel board where she'd drawn three columns and a timetable with a marker. In each box it said *Crafts, Swimming, Lunch, Feed pigs/sheep, Weed the vegetable garden, Hike, Clean the barn,* or *Free time* in big, cheerful handwriting. "We have a schedule." Lydia's nose wrinkled, and a few of the campers laughed.

Yuan cupped her hands over her mouth. "But this year we're sticking to it!" she joked.

Gabriela leaned over to Caro. "She always makes that schedule, but we end up just doing whatever we want every day. If it's warm we swim, if everyone's feeling lazy we do crafts. Usually the groups do different activities, but sometimes Lydia puts us all together."

"You think I'm joking," Lydia said, "but every one of your parents wrote on their forms that they want you *outside* in nature, doing things around the farm. So we're going to be hiking and visiting the animals and exploring the farm, okay?"

"Do we have to?" Alyssa whined. "Can't we just hang out here? There's air-conditioning here."

Lydia gave Alyssa a stern look. "Your dad told me *especially* that he wanted you with the animals as much as possible. He says you spend too much time indoors and he was very glad for you to have some electronic-free time this summer."

"That's what he said last summer," Alyssa muttered.

Lydia ignored her and went on. "You kids know that this is my first summer running camp alone," she said seriously.

"What are we, invisible?" Josh joked, pointing back and forth between himself and Yuan.

Lydia smiled at them. "Not quite alone. But I want you all to know that having you kids here is what my husband would have wanted."

Carolina looked around at everyone else's long faces. No one had told her that Lydia had once had a husband.

"July and August were his favorite months of the year because of summer camp. So things may be a little hectic this summer, since it's only me, but I wouldn't have it any other way. I've hired another farmer, Brian, to help me for the summer, and my son, George, may drop in from time to time."

Caro noticed Lydia's face fall, a line of worry creasing her forehead as if *yes,* there was another way she might want it, but just as quickly Lydia brightened. "What do you say we all go for a hike? It's perfect weather for it, and I could use the walk."

Everyone clambered to their feet and Lydia held up her hands. "One more thing. Just promise me you'll all stay on the paths this summer, okay? You're free to explore during your free times, but *always* stay on the marked trails. Promise?"

The kids nodded solemnly, and Lydia frowned her worried frown again.

"We'll keep everyone on track, Lydia," Josh promised, leading the group back out the door. They cut across the playground and joined a path, wide and brown, that started at the barn on their left, then cut across the fields and pastures that seemed to stretch on and on, all the way to the farm's farthest pasture. Carolina breathed in deeply. The tall grass in the fields smelled sweet. The hikers passed the cow herd, and kids shouted excitedly. The cows in this herd were soft browns and rich blacks, and they moved placidly through the grass, chewing pensively.

The campers came to a wooden bridge that arched high above a shallow brook, and Jennifer sidled up next to Carolina. "This is Cooke's Hill." She pointed to the woods that sloped up beyond the brook. "My house is right on the other side. I could hike to camp, but my mom doesn't let me."

From across the brook, the woods on the hill looked

dense, as if every inch were covered with green leaves. It seemed like there would be no room to walk between the tree trunks. But as they drew closer and crossed the bridge, Carolina saw that the trees were actually more sparse, and a clearly marked trail wound through them and up the hill.

The camp counselors spread out among the pack of kids. Yuan brought up the back of the group, to make sure no one got left behind.

"Carolina! Back here!" Gabriela waved.

Reluctantly, Carolina turned toward the back of the group. "I've got to go walk with my cousin," she told Jennifer, and wove her way through the crowd of kids to where Gabriela and her friends were standing.

Daniel and Ben were so excited that they were constantly running ahead of the pack, and Josh kept having to call them back. Carolina craned her neck as they walked, trying to keep an eye on Dani, but there were too many kids ahead of them. Gabriela and Alyssa were talking about Chiquifancy.

"I bet if she had a concert in New York City we could convince my dad to drive us," Gabriela said. "It's only three hours."

"Could your dad convince *my* dad?" Alyssa asked. "He thinks that Chiquifancy is too mature for us." Alyssa swept her short hair up with her hand. "I want to grow out my hair and wear it like Chiqui, what do you think?"

Gabriela cocked her head to the side, slowing down to consider. "Maybe. I don't know if you and Chiqui have the same face shape."

Alyssa let her hair fall and stuck out her tongue. "Not all of us were born looking exactly like Chiqui, Gabs. Some of us have to try. And, you know, *convince our parents.*"

"Okay, fine, I'll tell my dad he has to mention it to your parents."

"Deal." Alyssa turned to Jamie and demonstrated her updo again. "What do you think, Jams?"

Jamie barely looked. "It looks great, Alyssa! I love it! Really, really great."

Satisfied, Alyssa adjusted her pink barrette and led the way back up the hill, chattering about her plans to go see Chiquifancy in New York.

Carolina tried to look interested for Gabriela's sake. It was true, now that Alyssa mentioned it, that Gabriela looked a lot like Chiquifancy. She had the same black hair, the same body shape, even the line of her jaw was similar. The only difference was that Gabriela was lighter than Chiqui, who had the same tan skin as Mami and Daniel, who were just a shade darker than Caro. But when the conversation turned to concert tickets and hairstyles, Carolina tuned them out, barely noticing the climb until they reached the top of the hill and came to a clearing with a view of the farm below. From where they stood, the fields looked smooth, like patchwork scraps of green and brown, and the camp center looked like a Lego block. A wooden fence marked the drop at the edge of the clearing, and Carolina crouched so she could get a better view through the rails.

She imagined she was airborne, soaring over the farm,

and when the group headed back down the hill, she was the last one, straggling behind and letting her mind wander. She noticed tiny details in the woods, like clumps of moss and vines creeping up tree trunks. Carolina thought the moss and the vines looked somehow familiar, that if she asked them, they would know Puerto Rico, know it as closely and intimately as she did. *Mangroves, palms, lizards,* they would say. *Oh yes, those are our cousins, our dear cousins.* Carolina watched a squirrel leap from branch to branch, and felt a pull, as if every leap were drawing her farther from here, from New York, and deeper into her memory of home.

When she looked back down the trail, the group was gone.

Carolina sped up, hoping everyone else was just around the bend, or that she would hear their voices.

"Hello? Yuan? *Daniel!*"

There was no answer. Carolina hurried ahead, but the faster she went, the quieter the woods seemed to get, until she realized that she wasn't sure she was even on the trail— she might have just been making her own winding way through the trees. She hadn't noticed what the trail markers looked like, and now the path didn't seem clear at all. She wondered how long she'd have to be lost in the woods before they sent out a search party, and what Mami would say if she had to be rescued on her first day.

Carolina forced herself to breathe, turning in place and surveying everything around her. Cooke's Hill was pretty steep, and the one thing she was sure of was which way was up and which way was down. So she would head down, then. She didn't think she had any other choice.

She was focusing intently on the ground, picking exactly where to put her feet at each step, when she heard wind chimes jingling. Carolina stopped in place. The breeze was gentle, and stirred only a few flyaway strands of her hair, but it was enough for this jingle-jangle: musical, peaceful, and alluring, all at once. Each time she heard it, Carolina was back at home, back in her yard in Puerto Rico, listening to the call of the birds, the swish of the goldfish, the trickle of running water—and the wind chimes, playing the same notes in these hills that they had played from the terraza at home.

She forgot about feeling guilty and turned up the hill, toward the sound of the chimes. She reached the top and started walking down the other direction. There was a graceful slope in this direction; it wasn't nearly as steep here. The wind blew again, and again came the sound.

Through the trees, Carolina saw something blue, flapping lightly to the rhythm of the wind. She moved toward it, until she could see it was a tarp, taped onto the window of a tiny wooden house.

Carolina stood a few paces away, hanging on to the trunk of a tree, though the hill wasn't steep here, and she didn't really need the support.

The house was made of white clapboard, and the trimming had once been green, though now the paint was peeling off in long curls. From the back, a stone chimney rose like a vein in the center. On either side of the chimney was a window, one made of glass, and the other covered by the tarp. The jingling was coming from the other side, from what must be the front of the house, so she circled around, forcing herself not to look inside until she rounded the corner.

On this side there was a tiny pond, totally green and spotted with last autumn's fallen leaves. It shone where the light filtered through the trees and touched its surface. Someone had laid six rows of burnt-orange tiles in front of the little house. They were cracked and dusted with dirt, but to Carolina they evoked a place where a rocking chair might have been; where someone might have sat and looked at the pond. She moved toward the little patio, and there were the three silver chimes, hanging from a single stick on a hook by the front door. Carolina touched them lightly with her finger, knocking them together for a louder, rippling sound.

The door squeaked but yielded easily when Carolina reached out and pushed it open.

There was just one room inside, completely empty but for a metal grate in the fireplace. The floor was made of wide wooden planks. Where Carolina could see through the layer of dirt, the wood had turned gray and green in patches. The whole room was filled with a bluish green glow from the tarp, which flapped again and threatened to come loose from the window but didn't. Carolina idly wondered who had taped it up.

She lowered herself to the floor and rested her back against the cool walls. The dirt on the planks was damp and clung to her jeans, but she listened to the wind chimes and dreamed of who might have lived here, who else might have loved this little house—because Carolina knew that she was completely in love. She had thought she would never find another place she would love as much as her yard in Puerto Rico, but she had been wrong. No one could fail to love this perfect little place.

She thought an elderly woman would have fit well, one who sat in a rocking chair and looked at the pond. Or a legion of fairies, except this little house was too domestic, too neat for the wild fairies. *Elves,* Carolina thought. Maybe they visited, and burned a fire for Saint John, come midsummer.

She stayed as long as she dared, until her stomach rumbled and she remembered that this was not her house, that she was trespassing in the woods and Lydia would be counting heads soon and wondering where she was. *I'll be back,* she told herself, and shut the door behind her.

The woods felt familiar now, and knowing she'd gone down the wrong way, she climbed the short distance to the top of the hill, then headed down toward the farm confidently, until the ground leveled out and she could see the water of the brook dividing the pastures from the woods. She heard a whistle blowing, and hurried in its direction. The others were just reaching the bridge when she found them, and she slipped into the pack.

Chapter Three

Gabriela grabbed Carolina by the elbow as soon as they got back to the playground.

"Where did you go?" she hissed. "Look at you!"

Carolina pulled her arm free. "Nowhere."

Gabriela put her hands on her hips. "Nowhere. That's how you got covered in dirt? Going nowhere?"

Carolina tried to wipe some of the dust and dirt off of her shirt, but only rubbed it in farther. Mami was going to kill her—she'd starched and ironed all of Carolina's T-shirts before packing them. She thought it would help Carolina make a good impression.

"What's going on?" Alyssa shrieked. "Eww, there's a cobweb in your hair, Carolina!"

Jamie reached over and pulled the stretchy mess out of Carolina's hair. "It's off, Alyssa, relax. We were just in the woods, remember?"

Alyssa shook herself. "Ick. I can't stand that stuff. Good thing this camp only goes to thirteen. My parents would send me here forever if they could. They just think it's *so great* that I'm getting outside in the summer."

"Look, I'll talk to you later, okay?" Carolina spotted Jennifer by the swing set and started in her direction.

Gabriela threw her hands in the air. "You're really not going to tell me?"

Carolina ignored her and hurried toward Jennifer. "Hey, can I talk to you?"

"Sure." Jennifer hauled herself up to the clubhouse part of the swings, and Carolina followed suit. They sat with their legs dangling off the edge of the platform.

"You spend a lot of time here, right?" Carolina said finally.

Jennifer lay back on the platform. "Lydia lets me hang out here whenever I want, since we're neighbors. When everyone leaves in the afternoon, I sit up here and look at the clouds for a while. I think clouds are more like some*ones* than some*things*. I name all of the clouds I see. That's my inspiration."

Jennifer's words gave Carolina the chills. It was as if Jennifer had somehow read her inside and out, and she was telling Carolina a story about her own self. A story about sitting, just being. Their yard in Puerto Rico had been sprawling, with little stone paths that led back through the trees. Carolina used to take her sketchbook out there and sit beneath a flamboyán tree. It was her special spot, and she would sketch, and dream, and imagine what she would paint the next time she went to Señora Rivón's for art lessons.

Daniel had known not to bother her there, and so her special spot had been all peace—Qué descansada vida, as Papi said—sitting beneath the flamboyán with the wind chimes jingling in her ears. Jennifer understood.

"What do you do with the inspiration?" Carolina asked.

"I make art." Jennifer pulled something out of her pocket and dropped it into Carolina's hands.

Carolina pulled it toward her slowly. It was small, and fit snugly in her palm.

"You don't have to be so dainty. I made it sturdy."

It was a cradle, but it wouldn't have fit any doll Carolina knew of, only maybe a thimble, or a marble. It was painted to look like vines and flowers were growing all over it, painted so perfectly that Carolina nearly didn't believe that Jennifer, blaring with her multicolored braces, could have made anything so quiet and small.

But she had, Carolina knew. The cradle was sweet at the same time it was wild, and that was like Jennifer had been this morning, friendly but zany. Carolina felt as if she had found the missing pawn in a set after searching the entire toy bin, and she didn't want to let the cradle go.

"Who sleeps in it?"

"Elves, of course." Jennifer took back the cradle and pocketed it. "My dad had to help me with some of the carving, but just because my mom thought I might get cut."

Carolina sighed. "It's wonderful." She took a deep breath. "Jennifer—if your house is on the other side of Cooke's Hill, then I guess you've been to the top of the hill, right?"

"Of course I have. We were just there today, remember?"

Carolina shook her head. "I mean the top of the hill on the *other* side. Heading back down—you'd have to hike *up* from your house to get there."

Jennifer wiped her hands on her jeans. "Oh. Is that where you went? Yuan thought you were in the front with your brother." She hesitated. "You know we aren't really supposed to go that deep into the woods, right? Lydia doesn't like it."

"I didn't mean to go there," Carolina explained. "It was an accident."

"I love the woods," Jennifer said. "If it were up to me, kids would spend all day there, underneath the trees." She wrinkled her brow, scowling at the sky. "Do you know about Lydia's husband?"

"I know she had a husband." Carolina recalled Lydia's speech earlier in the camp day. "He liked kids."

"Paul. He was my favorite. You could go and sit in the barn and talk to him while he worked, and he didn't even expect you to help. Now Lydia just has Brian and her grown-up son, George, helping her, and they never talk to anyone."

Carolina gulped. "What happened to Paul?" But she knew the answer already, knew from Jennifer's stormy face what she was about to say.

"He died," Jennifer said matter-of-factly. "He was clearing a tree way back in the woods and he slipped on a ledge. That's why we're not supposed to go off the trail. Not that my parents ever let me go that far in the first place."

Carolina was speechless, imagining Paul—a man gray-haired like Lydia, strong and friendly—sprawled out on a bed of pine needles and dead leaves. It made her stomach flop.

Jennifer rolled over to face Carolina. "What did you see back there? Was it something incredible? Were you scared?" Jennifer seemed to have set aside the sadness from a minute ago, and now she asked questions eagerly. "Were there wild animals back there? I mean, of course there weren't any wild animals, but there *might* have been, you never know—"

"My mom would say you have an overactive imagination." Then, scared for a minute, Carolina asked, "*Are* there wild animals back there?"

"No," Jennifer answered promptly. "Well. Deer. Lots and lots of deer."

"So then—"

Jennifer shrugged. "You never know."

"I did find something," Carolina said boldly. She told Jennifer about the little green pond, and the wind chimes, and finally, all in a rush, she told her about the tiny house and what she had imagined—the old woman in the rocking chair, and the elves tidying up at night. "I thought maybe you knew something about the cabin—like why it's there, or who it belongs to."

Jennifer shook her head slowly. "I've never heard about it. No one told me." She sat up and hugged her knees. "I bet no one even knows it's there. The woods are full of abandoned places. We could even fix it up!" Jennifer's eyes were shining, and she clasped her hands over her heart. "Can we go see it?"

"Won't we get in trouble?"

Jennifer grabbed Carolina's hand. "Come over after camp next week. Come on Tuesday. My mom works late on Tuesdays, and my dad won't bother us."

After camp, Carolina went straight to her desk in her room and closed the door. She turned to a blank page in her sketchbook and drew clouds, using the side of her pencil to shade them in. She tried to make them seem round and fluffy instead of flat. If the drawing came out well, she'd show it to Jennifer.

"Can I come in?" Gabriela stood in the doorway.

"Oh. You don't have to ask." Carolina closed her sketchbook quickly. Gabriela hadn't said a word to her on the car ride home. "I just took a wrong turn during the hike. I didn't go anywhere," Carolina lied.

"Don't be friends with Jennifer," Gabriela blurted out.

"Huh?"

"She's nice and all, but did you *look* at her? She's totally nuts."

Carolina could feel heat charge up her neck. "I didn't think she was nuts. Who cares what she looks like?"

"Seriously?" Gabriela shut the door and sat down on the bed. "Everyone cares what she looks like—why does she have to dress that way? One of these days there's going to be an animal in that braid instead of a paintbrush."

"Her dad's a painter, and she likes to make art. What's the big deal?"

Gabriela crossed her arms. "Look, Carolina, I'm trying to be nice to you, because you're new here. But everyone in all of Larksville knows that Jennifer is a weirdo, and so is her artist dad. Wait until you see their house. When we lived over on that side of town we would drive by it sometimes, and it's a wreck."

Carolina shrugged and opened up her sketchbook again. "I'm going there next week."

"You don't get it. We already stick out in Larksville—in case you hadn't noticed, it's not like there are tons of other Puerto Ricans walking around here."

Carolina said nothing. If that was the problem, she didn't know what she was supposed to do about it. Gabriela was half-white; she could ignore the Puerto Rican half sometimes. But she, Carolina, was all Puerto Rican, all the time. Then she had a thought. "Chiquifancy is Puerto Rican."

"That's different, she's cool," Gabriela retorted. "Don't you even care what people think?"

Carolina felt tears gathering, and wished they wouldn't. Gabriela was probably thinking what a baby she was. She pressed her eyes with the heel of her hand.

There was a knock, and Mami pushed the door open. "Papi and Uncle Porter just—" She noticed Gabriela, then

Carolina's face. "What's wrong? Have you two been fighting? It's only been one day!"

Gabriela crossed her arms and didn't answer.

Mami did a double take. "Caro! You're filthy!" She looked back and forth between Gabriela and Carolina, confused. "They said you might get dirty, but—you're muddier than Daniel! Did you fall into a pigsty?"

Gabriela giggled, then straightened her face. "Tía Ana," she said seriously, "it's this girl at camp. Jennifer. She's a little—*unusual,* and Carolina went off with her today, I'm sure that's what it was."

Carolina shot Gabriela a look. *Thanks for nothing,* she thought to herself.

Mami threw her hands up. "You couldn't play with someone less messy?"

"We weren't *playing—*"

Mami raised her eyebrows and Carolina looked down at her shoes.

"Jennifer invited me to her house." She didn't dare look up.

"I see," Mami said, clearly torn. "You know I can't let you go to anyone's house until we know the parents, Caro."

"But, Mami, Jennifer's an artist," Carolina pleaded. "Just like me."

"Ay, Caro," Mami said. "Enough with the art. You should be socializing, and getting to know your cousin. It's the perfect opportunity for you and Gabs. I don't want you to spend so much time with your head in the clouds, mi vida." Mami took a deep breath. "I want you to have your playdate. But we're new here, and if Gabriela says there's something wrong with this girl—"

"There's nothing wrong with her!" Carolina exploded.

Gabriela grabbed her bag. "Fine. Hang out with whoever you want." She slammed the door behind her.

"Caro," Mami said disappointedly. "I don't want you talking to your cousin in that tone. You have to calm down, okay? Ven." Mami patted the bed, but Caro stayed in her chair. "Come on," Mami said coaxingly. "Tell me about camp! How was it?"

Carolina crossed her arms. She wasn't falling for Mami's pathetic attempt to distract her. "Gabriela was the one talking to *me* in that tone, Mami."

Mami shook her head. "It's her house, Caro."

"So?"

"So you have to be patient with her! Caro, I thought you wanted to help Papi and me. We're going through a lot right now, and Tía Cuca and her family are being very generous letting us stay here!"

"It's not like they could say no, not living in this mansion!"

"Lower your voice!" Mami looked over her shoulder, as if the size of the house were some kind of state secret. "They're being very nice, and you have to find a way to get along with your cousin," Mami hissed. She stood up and held the door open. "Can you please go talk to her?"

Carolina wanted to slam the door and stomp like Gabriela

had done, but she couldn't, and that was the most unfair part. She could hear the other grown-ups downstairs, and as much as she hated to admit it, she didn't want them to know that she and Gabriela had been fighting any more than Mami did. She knocked on Gabriela's door and allowed herself just one impatient foot tap.

"Come in."

Carolina pushed the door open. The room was a total mess. There were piles of magazines in every corner. A nail polish bottle had spilled, and the enamel had hardened on Gabriela's desk. Gabriela was sitting in the middle of the floor, typing on her laptop.

"Sorry."

"That's okay," Gabriela responded coolly. "I was just trying to help."

"That's all I had to say." Carolina turned to go.

"Wait!" Gabriela pushed her laptop aside and stood. "Look, if you want to go to Jennifer's, fine. Just— Don't advertise it, okay? Alyssa's my best friend, and she can't stand Jennifer always tagging behind us with her weird games." Gabriela scuffed the polished wood floor with her foot. "Besides, my parents and I only moved to this part of Larksville a little while ago. I don't want Alyssa to think that we still belong out in the backwoods."

"You have just as much a right to live in this part of town as Alyssa does," Carolina said.

"Not really. Alyssa's dad owns the real estate company my dad works for. They built all these houses."

{45}

"Oh." Carolina shook her head. "Still." She studied Gabriela, then took a deep breath. "But if it's what you really want, I won't say too much about Jennifer to your friends. Or I'll try, at least."

Gabriela picked her laptop up again. "Thanks." She flashed Carolina a small smile.

It was lucky that Tía Cuca could talk for several people at once, because Carolina didn't feel like saying much when she went downstairs to help set the table. They sat down to eat early, because Tía Cuca said that was when Uncle Porter liked his dinner.

"Everyone here eats early," Mami said, as if she had some kind of human antenna for what "people here" did.

Carolina muttered under her breath that she wasn't even hungry yet.

"Are you mad?" Daniel asked.

Carolina served him a helping of salad. "Not at you, silly. Just— I don't like that we have to do everything just like everyone else here. Have you noticed that?"

Daniel's eyes were big and wide. "Ben's parents make brussels sprouts three times a week, and he says they're disgusting. We're not going to have to start eating brussels sprouts three times a week, are we? Because if we are—"

"That's not what I meant, Daniel. You know, like other stuff."

"Like what?"

"Oh, forget it. It's not important."

Tía Cuca finished passing around the salad. "Okay, now tell us absolutely everything about camp today. How was it?"

Before anyone could answer, Carolina cleared her throat. "I was invited to someone's house."

Mami gulped down a swig of water, but Uncle Porter asked mildly, "That's nice. Whose house?"

"Her name is Jennifer. I don't— I didn't ask her last name," Carolina said.

"Murry," Gabriela volunteered.

"I told Caro we have to know the family before she can go anywhere, of course," Mami said. "She knows she can't go to strangers' houses."

Uncle Porter chewed his meat thoughtfully. "Murry. Do we know them?"

"You know her, Daddy," Gabriela supplied. "She's the one who always has that stuff in her hair."

Mami's eyebrows shot up.

Uncle Porter slapped his knee. "Oh yeah! Jennifer! Her mom works at the diner; we see her there sometimes. And the dad's an artist, a little washed up, I think. I know Jennifer, she's a character. You kids will have a great time."

Mami looked back and forth between him and Gabriela. "So, Porter, are they good people? I don't want to let Carolina play with someone if they're from a bad family or—"

Uncle Porter reached for his wine. "She should go! It's great that you have a friend so soon, Caro."

Gabriela slumped in her seat, but Carolina grinned broadly. Mami would never stop something that Uncle Porter was so enthusiastic about.

Carolina slid open the glass door and let herself out onto the deck. The yard was filled with earthy hues: the deep brown cedar of the deck and the orange of the sun, which drifted still lower on its June journey through the sky. There were marigolds growing in the little planters that hung on the rail, and a brown bunny hopped across the grass below. Carolina went down a few steps to the grassy part of the yard and opened her sketchbook. She wanted to finish her cloud drawing in time to show it to Jennifer tomorrow.

She'd barely started the second cloud when she heard the sliding glass door again. Uncle Porter came out carrying a newspaper, Gabriela not far behind with her phone.

"Don't let us bother you," he called, unfolding his newspaper.

Neither of them was looking at her. But still, Carolina felt like she was on a stage, the only thing sticking out of this flat trim lawn. She longed for her own yard and the cover of her flamboyán tree.

When she looked up again, Papi was coming down the steps toward her. He wore khakis and a white linen shirt, crisp and light for the sun.

"Why so sad, Caro?" He sat down next to her in the grass, as if he didn't mind at all, sitting like this where anyone could see them, didn't mind at all that his khakis rode up as he attempted, clumsily, to sit cross-legged.

"It's just . . ." Her voice faded as she searched for words. "Mami's changed," she said finally. "She never cared before whether I was popular, and she used to *like* it when I talked about art."

"Mami just wants things to work out here," Papi said. "She wants to show your tía Cuca and uncle Porter that we appreciate everything they're doing for us, and that we're making an effort."

Carolina pressed down with her pencil, leaving a deep gray impression on the page. "I am making an effort. I can't help it if I don't think everything is perfect all the time."

Papi patted her back. "I know you're sad, Caro. So am I. Do you know that, my Carolinita? I miss home as much as you do."

"You do?" Carolina sniffed. They were speaking Spanish, and she wondered if Papi missed that, too—being able to speak Spanish whenever they wanted, like they could at home. Here, Carolina spoke Spanish only when she was alone with her parents or Dani.

"It isn't easy to leave. But we'll be happy here, you'll see."

Caro let Papi's words fall over her, then wash away. "Can't we just keep the house?" she asked. "Maybe you'll get another job in Puerto Rico and then you'll have sold our whole house for no reason."

She let her questions trail away, knowing there was no answer that Papi could give her, no answer she'd want to hear.

"Will we—will we ever go back?"

"Caminante, no hay camino," Papi said.

"Traveler, there is no path," Carolina quoted. The words to this poem were written on her heart, she knew them perfectly. *"You make your path by walking. . . . Traveler, there is no path, only your wake upon the sea."* Carolina wiped her eyes. It was Papi's favorite poem, written by a Spanish poet named Antonio Machado. At home, Papi had liked to play a version of the poem set to music. He hummed it now, and for the second time that day Carolina thought of the sea and of the pastures stretching on and on. The melody soothed her and made home feel closer, as if every mile of field and sea were connected.

"When your grandparents came to Puerto Rico from Cuba," Papi said, "they didn't know what would happen to them. They couldn't plan everything out."

It made Carolina dizzy, thinking of all these moves— her family leaving Cuba and starting a new life in Puerto Rico, and now this, another move, another new beginning. Papi's parents had left Cuba long before he'd been born, but Mami's family had gone to Puerto Rico when Mami was little, and she still remembered some things about Cuba. It was like a game of hopscotch, jumping island to island, and now all the way to upstate New York, with no plans to return. She thought it would break her grandparents' hearts, if they were alive to know: all that for nothing, all that to move once more.

"We'll have to be like Antonio Machado," Papi said. "We'll make our path by walking." He put one arm around Caro, and hummed "Caminante, no hay camino" to himself, while around them squirrels jostled through leaves and hedges, and a sprinkler watered the lawn next door, back and forth.

Chapter Four

Caro liked the smell of fresh hay and the dusty shade of the barn, and noticed how sweaty she'd gotten only as she and the rest of her camp group stepped outside. It was the second week of camp, and the day was hot and muggy.

"So," Yuan said, coming up beside Carolina. "First barn cleaning a success?"

"I liked it," Caro said shyly.

"You liked it?" Alyssa said, walking backward down the path so that she faced Caro. "How is that even possible?"

"A lot of people do," Jennifer said simply. "It's like we're making a home for the animals to come back to."

Carolina shrugged, trying to appear noncommittal, for Gabriela's sake.

Yuan pulled a rumpled piece of paper out of her pocket. "Our group is supposed to go to the greenhouse now. Come on." She waved them forward.

"Paul never made me do anything," Alyssa said suddenly. "That's right," she went on. "He told me that just because he was a farmer didn't mean I had to like farming to be a good camper, or his friend."

"He used to let us hang out in the camp center, remember?" Gabriela said.

"And make us those apple slices," Jamie added. "He cut them so thin you could see the sun shine through."

"He made those when I was a camper here too," Yuan said with a smile.

Carolina skipped a little as she made her way down the lane. There was something glorious about Silver Meadows, about the rich scent of mud and grass all around.

"Remember his fishing vest?" Jamie asked the others.

"Oh yeah!" Gabriela said. "Lydia hated it. She thought he looked silly."

Jennifer grinned. "But do you remember what was in the pockets?"

They reached the place where the path passed the playground, and slowed down. The younger kids were busy with tetherball and the monkey bars. Lydia was pushing Lisa, one of the little girls, on the swings.

Dani ran up to Carolina's group, Ben close behind him. "Caro! Caro!"

Gabriela held her hand out over the playground's wooden fence, and Dani and Ben both high-fived her. It was like they'd all known each other for years, Caro thought, high-fiving and joking like old friends.

"What were you-all talking about?" Dani climbed onto

the bottom rung of the fence and held on at the top, leaning into the path.

"We were talking about Paul," Jennifer answered. "You never met him, but this was his farm. His and Lydia's."

"Aw, I loved Paul!" Ben chimed in. "He used to give me erasers."

"Erasers?" Caro asked.

Jennifer's braid swung as she talked, tapping the fence like a pendulum. "In his fishing vest. It was full of treasures. Gum and marbles and erasers shaped like animals—he always had something. Once, I made him a tiny fairy, and he carried it in his pocket for a week," Jennifer said proudly.

"*Shhhh.*" Jamie elbowed Jennifer and pointed toward Lydia, who was headed toward them. "It might make her sad."

Abruptly, Alyssa changed the subject. "Hey," she said as Lydia reached the playground. "How come the little kids get free time and we don't?"

Lydia laughed.

"Please?" Jennifer begged, on Alyssa's team for once. "I'm working on a new craft project."

"Well . . ."

"I'll spend some time outside," Jennifer promised, following Lydia's gaze to the open pastures, blooming with chicory and clover.

"Deal," Lydia agreed, and Alyssa, Gabriela, and Jamie tore off to the air-conditioned camp center.

"I'll go get my craft stuff and bring it out here," Jennifer said.

Caro stood by herself on the path. In the sunlight, Cooke's

Hill shone a brilliant green, and Carolina found herself thinking of the abandoned cabin in the woods. She wondered if anyone had ever lived there, and if they would mind if Carolina borrowed it for her own, just for a summer. In her mind's eye, Carolina saw elves dancing on the tile, and she saw herself, right at home. She put one foot in front of the other, her heart racing as she moved farther down the lane that cut through the pasture.

"Carolina?" Lydia called, and Caro stopped in her tracks. She turned back to the playground. Jennifer lingered halfway between the fence and the camp center, watching them.

"Yes?" Caro asked with a squeak.

"Stay on the paths, okay?" Lydia said.

Jennifer ducked under the fence and stood by Caro. "I'll stay with her so she knows where she's going."

"That goes for you, too, Jennifer." Lydia's face meant business. "I want you girls on the trails and out of harm's way. Okay? *Okay?*"

"Okay." Jennifer and Carolina nodded, and Lydia returned to the swings, satisfied.

"We'll have to wait until we get to my house tomorrow," Jennifer said when they were alone. "Lydia's got her eye on us today."

When Tuesday rolled around, Carolina was nearly bursting with excitement. She was going to meet a painter, and she was going to see the cabin, her off-the-trail and out-of-bounds beloved cabin.

Jennifer's dad picked them up after camp in his truck. "Hi, Jenn!" he said from the driver's seat. "Hop on back!"

Carolina followed Jennifer into the fold-down seats. Her knees bumped the back of the front seat, and she was glad she wasn't any taller. She peered around at Jennifer's dad as he pulled out of the Silver Meadows parking lot and turned onto the main road. His gray hair was pulled back into a ponytail, and Carolina noticed paint splatters on the thighs of his jeans.

"Nice to meet you," Jennifer's dad said to her. "I'm Gavin."

"Hi, Gavin," Carolina said shyly. She leaned back and hugged her knees. She was in a truck with an artist, a real artist.

They were on the main road for only a moment before they turned again, onto a narrow dirt road so closely surrounded by trees that even the sky looked green. Carolina wondered if this was what Uncle Porter and Tía Cuca's road had been like, before it had been paved over and lined with new houses.

When they pulled into the driveway, Jennifer unbuckled her seat belt and raced to her front door, but Carolina lingered. Jennifer's house was the only one for as far as Carolina could see. The lawn had a vegetable garden, with leafy tomato vines crawling up a trellis, and timothy grass rustled noisily beyond the garden.

Then there were the sculptures. Everywhere were twisting sculptures of mosaic glass and old, colorful bottles. Jennifer's front yard was a hodgepodge of grass growing wild, cheerful vegetables, and sparkling artwork.

"Hurry up!" Jennifer motioned for Carolina to come in. "We've got a lot to do!"

Gavin disappeared into his studio at the back of the house as soon as they got there, and Jennifer led Carolina up to her room.

"That's the great thing about my dad," Jennifer explained. "If I need help with a project he's always right here at home, but he doesn't bother me if I don't need anything. My mom on the other hand . . ." Jennifer grimaced.

"I know what you mean." Carolina savored the uneven wooden staircase. Each step was wide, and the wood undulated in the middle, where a hundred years of feet had stepped. Jennifer's house *breathed;* the air in here was the same air from outside, cool but not cold. The house smelled like fresh soil, and Carolina breathed it in deep.

Jennifer flung open the door to her room. "Ta-da!"

It was like its own little studio, taken up mostly by a folding table piled with baskets of colorful wool roving, jars of acorn caps, and scraps of fabric.

"Is this where you do your art?" Carolina stared hungrily at Jennifer's table, which almost groaned under the weight of all the art supplies.

"Yeah! Ever made anything from felt? I could teach you."

"Not from felt." Carolina cleared her throat, which was suddenly scratchy. "But I paint. I—I mean," she stammered, "draw. I like both. But right now I draw."

Her face burned, but Jennifer took everything in stride. "Do you have a sketchbook? Did you bring it?"

Carolina patted her backpack silently.

"Show me when we go to the cabin. I have some stuff I want to bring too." Jennifer pulled a long plastic storage container from under her bed.

Carolina's jaw dropped. Dozens of small felt statues stared up at her. "Did you make all those?"

"Of course I did, who else would have made them?" Jennifer reached in and pulled out one of the tiny dolls, with its acorn cap and floral skirt. "At first it was really hard for me to make the little skirts; I used to use glue, but now I can sew them and they look more real, don't you think?"

Carolina marveled at the little doll. "Why are they all in here? Why don't you take them out?"

Jennifer ran her tongue over her braces. After a while, she said, "I could. I used to have them all over the house. I liked putting them in all the nooks and crannies—this house is full of good hiding spots. But now that I'm starting middle school . . ."

"What does middle school have to do with it?"

"My mom says I'm too old for dolls. I tried telling her that they're not dolls, they're elves, but that made her even more worried. She told me to stop leaving them all over the place."

"Wow." Carolina ran her fingernail over the ridged fabric of her backpack strap. "Sometimes my mom thinks I'm too old for drawing, and for talking about fairies. She thinks I need to socialize more, like with Gabriela and her friends."

"And talk about Chiquifancy all day?" Jennifer wrinkled her nose. "No thank you." Carefully, Jennifer stacked several of the elves into her camp bag. She hoisted the bag up on her knee and peered inside. "I've got everything. Let's go."

Carolina followed Jennifer back down the stairs, to her dad's sunlit studio. Jennifer threw her arms around his neck. "Daddy, can Carolina and I go outside?"

Carolina noticed that Gavin had a folding table just like Jennifer's, piled with coffee cans and yogurt containers full of brushes, pens, and paints. It smelled like Señora Rivón's studio. Carolina scanned the shelves, ogling the bottles and bottles of paint. Several canvases leaned against the wall, many of them wrapped in brown paper. One was face out, unwrapped. Carolina moved closer to it.

The painting showed the sea, aquamarine and sparkling. Brushstrokes swirled on the canvas. It moved with a rhythm and a beauty that was familiar even as it was different. Carolina didn't know if Gavin had ever even been to Puerto Rico, and yet she was certain that this sea was the Caribbean. It was the sea of her parents and grandparents and Carolina herself, of Cuba and Puerto Rico. What brush could create this sweeping sensation? With every fiber of her being, Carolina wanted to be like Gavin.

He tugged on Jennifer's braid playfully. "Just stay on the trail, okay?"

As if on cue, Carolina started coughing, unable to stop

herself. Jennifer elbowed her. "Deal," she told her dad, and dragged Carolina toward the back door.

"What are you doing, trying to give us away?" Jennifer complained as soon as they were out of earshot.

Carolina sputtered. "I've just— I don't think I've ever— Well, I just feel bad. We lied to your dad."

Jennifer shrugged. "I like exploring the woods. Besides, I want to see the cabin."

Carolina chewed on her nail as they left Jennifer's house. There was a path leading into the woods just feet away from the back door, and Jennifer led the way. Carolina took her hand out of her mouth and stuck it in her pocket. Mami hated it when she bit her nails; she said it was rude. Carolina looked over her shoulder.

"Relax!" Jennifer took a half-eaten granola bar out of her bag and offered Carolina a bite. "They'll never know we weren't three feet away from the house the whole time."

Carolina took the granola bar, and they munched and walked until they came to the spot where the trail ended, and all around were trees.

Jennifer stopped abruptly. "This is as far as I usually come."

Carolina turned in place. "You mean the trail just ends?"

"Yep, this is it. You remember which direction the cabin is, right?"

"I guess so." Carolina examined the trees just beyond the cleared path. "Not exactly El Yunque," she muttered under her breath.

"What's that?

Carolina shook her head. "It's a rainforest in Puerto Rico. Where I'm from."

"Neat." Jennifer opened her mouth as if she wanted to say something else, then closed it.

"We keep hiking up, I guess?"

Jennifer twisted her backpack around to the front. "Luckily I came prepared." She pulled a roll of ribbon and a small pair of scissors from her bag, and tied a ribbon to the nearest branch. "We have to mark our turns, otherwise we could be lost up there forever."

"Like Hansel and Gretel."

"Only smarter." Jennifer tapped her forehead to show her intelligence. "Ribbons don't get eaten by birds."

They walked through the woods, tying ribbons every few feet. They reached a place where the slope of the hill was gentle, and climbed more quickly, but still there was no sign of the cabin. Carolina was giving up hope, convinced she would never see it again. Then the tinkling of the chimes filled her ears, and she tore off toward the sound.

"Slow down, Carolina! You're going to trip!"

Carolina hurried. "Come on! If we lose the track now we might never find it."

"Yeah, but there are living things in this forest," Jennifer hissed. "You're probably frightening them away by crashing around so much."

Carolina slowed down. "Isn't that a good thing?"

Jennifer caught up with her. "Not really. Just walk a little slower. I've never been up this far before. It feels . . . *weird,* to make so much noise."

They crept the rest of the way. Somewhere a branch cracked, and somewhere a bird sang, and they plunged forward until they were standing in front of the green pond, looking at the house and its burnt-orange tile porch.

Jennifer stood very straight. For once, her braid ran down the center of her back, not swinging or moving at all. "Oh," she said. "Oh."

Carolina hugged her elbows. "Do you—do you like it?"

"It's perfect," Jennifer whispered. "Can we go inside?"

Like she was welcoming Jennifer into her own house, Carolina stepped over the tiles and pushed open the door. It was just as she'd left it. The blue tarp was still in its window, the floor still showed impressions in the dust where her feet had walked.

Jennifer spun slowly in place. "What is this place? This house must have been someone's, at some point." She went back to the door and stood in the entry. "I can't believe I've never been here before. It's practically in my backyard."

"It's so small that it gets hidden by the trees."

"Do you think someone ever lived here?" Jennifer went to the empty fireplace. "I mean, it's all one room, but it has a fireplace. Someone could have stayed here."

"I don't know." Carolina didn't like to think about that; she already thought of this house as belonging to her—and to the elderly woman she'd imagined.

Carolina squatted in front of the empty fireplace. "I

thought from the first time I came here that it was the perfect place for elves. I didn't know you had made those elf dolls."

Jennifer's eyes sparkled. She took an elf out of her pocket, a green-clad wool figure with an acorn cap as his hat, and placed him in the center of the fireplace. She lifted one of his wire arms, as if he were waving hello.

"Hello," Carolina said, waving back. "Hola."

They lay on the floor after that and listened to the sounds of the house: the hoot of a bird, the *swish, swish* of the trees that surrounded them. Carolina wondered if Jennifer was collecting inspiration. She closed her eyes and let herself sink down into a memory that hit her as the chimes jingled outside: of waking up in her old bedroom, with the swoop of the overhead fan. She imagined the cool sweep, then the still hotness, pausing, then coming again. She thought of humidity, seeping into her before she'd even awoken. *Qué descansada vida,* she thought. *What a peaceful life.*

"Carolina?"

"Hmmm?"

"Are there elves in Puerto Rico?"

Carolina rolled onto her side and propped herself up with her elbow. "They're called duendes. I had a book about them, when I was little."

"Good."

A solitary drop of rain hit the roof of the house. It was a lovely sound. Carolina liked sitting here quietly, bathed in the bluish green light that filtered in through the tarp on the window. More drops of rain fell, rhythmic and soft. It wasn't like the great downpours of home, and it wasn't monotonous, like all-day rain. It was just-right rain.

Carolina dragged her backpack toward her and pulled out her sketchbook. She flipped to her clouds and slid the sketchbook toward Jennifer. "I drew these for you."

Jennifer sat up and examined the clouds. "These are great, Carolina. Are you going to paint them?"

Carolina took the book back and flipped through her drawings. "I don't think so. At home I had oil painting classes, but I don't think I'm going to have them here." Then she added, "Not until my parents find new jobs, at least."

Jennifer pulled a length of bendable wire from her backpack and started shaping it into a stick figure. "My dad gives private classes sometimes." She shook out the contents of her backpack and rummaged through the tufts of wool roving and scraps of fabric for some brown wool, which she padded onto her figure's legs.

"That's cool." Carolina tried to look nonchalant and pulled her pencils out from her own backpack. Thankfully, Jennifer didn't seem to want to talk more about it, so Carolina leaned against the wall and turned to a blank page. She thought about drawing the sea, but she knew she couldn't imitate what Gavin had done, not with pencil and paper and maybe not for years and years. Painting well took practice, Señora Rivón had always told her. Still, she wanted to draw something that spoke to her like the sea did, and she moved her pencil to the bottom of the page, drawing the roots of a tree on the far left, then the leaves spreading out to the right in an enormous canopy.

Jennifer straightened up from her felting and cocked her head to the side. "You know, Carolina, you don't need oil paint to add colors." She rummaged through her bag and pulled out a red pen. "What about pens?"

Caro weighed the pen in her hand. "Yeah," she said slowly. "Maybe." She tucked the red pen into her backpack.

Jennifer glanced at her watch. "We should probably start hiking back. We don't want to be late for your mom."

"We'll be in huge trouble if we're out of bounds when she gets here," Carolina agreed.

Jennifer repacked her bag and tapped the acorn cap of the elf in the fireplace. "Good-bye, little guy," she said. "See you soon."

The sound of the leaves grew suddenly louder as a breeze blew through the cabin.

"That tarp!" Carolina ran over and pushed down the loose edge so it wouldn't fly away. Jennifer pressed down the other side.

Thoughtfully, Carolina looked up at the window. "You know, if we're going to come back here—"

"We are. Definitely."

"Maybe we could make some curtains."

Jennifer examined the windows. "That would be so, so cozy. Except I don't have that much fabric."

Carolina considered the problem. "I think my tía Cuca likes to sew, or used to. I could ask her."

"And there's always sheets," Jennifer added.

Carolina fingered the tarp, then stepped back to take in the whole cabin, the chimney and the fireplace and the windows, one covered in a tarp, the other with glass. She could imagine the curtains perfectly: cheerful and yellow, rustling in the wind, keeping rhythm with the chimes. And Jennifer's elf in the fireplace, the little duende, waiting to greet them each time they arrived. It was the perfect spot.

Chapter Five

They got back to Jennifer's house with just enough time for Carolina to change out of her muddy clothes. She put her backpack on Jennifer's bed and pulled out a clean pair of jeans, ones that still had creases in them from how Mami had folded them into her suitcase. She buried her face and took a long sniff.

Jennifer, who was sitting at her desk finishing another elf figurine, raised an eyebrow. "Your jeans smell good?"

Carolina peeled off her muddy pants. "Like starch." She rolled the pants into a neat ball and put them in the very bottom of her backpack. "They remind me of my old house. I think my tía Cuca must clean things differently than we did at home."

Mami came to pick her up, thanking Gavin with all her teeth showing. But as they made their way to the car, Carolina saw Mami's eyes linger on the front yard.

Carolina waved good-bye to Jennifer and followed Mami. Rain pattered onto the path, and each droplet turned the slate a dark charcoal that bloomed and spread over the stone. Mami's keys beeped as she fumbled to open Tía Cuca's car, and Carolina took one last look over her shoulder.

The mismatched yard looked bedraggled in the rain. The leaves in the vegetable garden drooped, and with no light for the sculptures to reflect, they didn't sparkle. Now she saw through Mami's eyes, and she wondered how long you had to go without mowing your lawn before it grew as long and wild as it did here. She climbed into the car and shut the door.

They drove out of the green tunnel of Jennifer's dirt road and turned onto the paved county route. "That's quite a house," Mami said.

"You don't like it." Carolina looked at her hands.

Mami flipped on the windshield wipers. "Cuca told me the dad's a painter; you'd think he'd paint his own house. It looks like the whole thing is falling down."

"He's not that kind of painter."

Almost to herself, Mami said, "They must be poor, still living out in the backwoods like that."

Carolina took her time unraveling Mami's words. She didn't think Jennifer was poor. It was true that her house was way out in the woods and everyone else in Larksville seemed to be moving to shiny new houses, but Carolina loved Jennifer's house. Then she thought back to the kids from her school in Puerto Rico. Carolina had never had a ton of friends, but she'd known everyone at her small Catholic school. She couldn't think of anyone from her old school whose dad had long hair and paint-splattered jeans.

"But we're poor, too, aren't we?" Carolina said finally. "I mean, since we moved here and Papi doesn't have a job."

Mami tsked. "That's temporary." She leaned forward over the steering wheel. "Mi vida, they seemed a little strange."

Carolina lifted her gaze and watched the rain hitting the hood of the car. "You never used to care what people's houses were like," Caro said. "Now you want to do whatever Tía Cuca and Uncle Porter do. They moved to a new house, and now you only like new houses."

Mami didn't take her eyes off the road. "I'm just trying to help you adjust," she said slowly. "Some of the things Cuca has told me, about when she first came to Larksville . . . And Gabriela was really excited to introduce you to Alyssa, and to her other friends."

"Well, what if I don't care about Gabriela's friends?" Carolina protested.

"Caro," Mami said, "I was very young when we left Cuba for Puerto Rico, but I still know what it's like to be new somewhere, to be different. When you're new, you care a lot about your family, about being close to them." Mami sighed. "You'll see." She lowered the speed of the windshield wipers as the rain slowed. "You should be grateful to have Gabriela to show you how things work around here."

Carolina stared out the window. The stretch of road in

this part of Larksville was surrounded by open country. She *was* grateful, she knew there were kids who had it so much worse, and yet she didn't see why family should stop her from coming to Jennifer's, from following the trail that led through the woods and up the hill, to the place where the cabin was tucked away.

"What did you and Jennifer do today, anyway?"

Carolina shifted in her seat. It was a good thing Mami couldn't see her ears, which were turning hot and red.

"Caro?" Mami prompted.

"We just talked." She felt around to make sure the dirty jeans were still deep in her backpack.

Mami looked up, examining Carolina through the rear-view mirror.

Carolina decided to test an idea that had been forming all afternoon. "Mami, do you think—maybe in a couple of months—do you think I could get painting lessons from Jennifer's dad? He gives lessons, you know."

They were getting to the only traffic light in Larksville, at the intersection with the sturdy brick post office and the steepled church whose wooden doors were painted bright red. Mami stopped at the traffic light and turned toward Carolina. "Mi amor—"

"Not now, I know lessons are expensive, just—someday."

Mami nodded. "Someday, you'll have art classes again. But you know, there might be another activity you want to do—or an art center in one of the other towns, a place where you could meet other kids your own age."

"I don't want to meet other kids. I want Jennifer's dad to teach me. Promise me you'll let me?" Carolina pleaded. "Someday?"

There was a hint of moisture in Mami's eyes, and she reached back and patted Carolina's cheek. "Okay, Carolinita. Someday."

The light changed, and Mami turned onto the gleaming new blacktop of Tía Cuca and Uncle Porter's street.

Uncle Porter was making iced tea from a powder mix. He rolled up the sleeves of his dress shirt and stirred the pitcher with a long wooden spoon. The rain had stopped, so Carolina slipped away to the deck and stretched out on one of the lawn chairs. Daniel followed her, and she had to get up again to shut the sliding door so that the cold air wouldn't escape the house. Daniel ran down the steps onto the grass. He crouched in the bushes and talked to the ants and squirrels. Carolina pulled her sketchbook out of her backpack and kept working on her tree. She noticed that the branches of the oaks all around her grew upward, closer to the sky, but the branches of Carolina's tree grew out to the side. She added blossoms. Then she reached into her backpack and found Jennifer's red pen. The blossoms burned red and came to life as Carolina filled them in with the pen.

"Papi!" Carolina jumped to her feet as Papi opened the sliding glass door, holding a cup of iced tea. She hugged him tight. "How was your day?"

"It was okay." He sounded tired. "I met with your uncle Porter's boss, Lance Rogan."

"Alyssa's dad," Carolina said. "Would you work for him too? Building houses?"

Papi shook his head. "No, but he knows a lot of people in the area. People who can help me get interviews and find other jobs."

Carolina didn't say anything else. Papi seemed distant, and worn-out. He opened a newspaper, and Carolina kept sketching.

After a time, Papi asked softly, "What's that you're drawing?"

Shyly, Carolina turned the book so Papi could see it. She hadn't shown him any of her artwork in weeks, not since the last class she'd had with Señora Rivón.

"A flamboyán?"

Carolina nodded.

Papi closed his eyes. "My father used to talk about the flamboyán in his yard in Cuba."

"And that's why you and Mami chose our house in Puerto Rico," Carolina added with a smile. "Because it had a flamboyán tree to remind you of Abuelo Titico."

Papi stared out over the deck, to where Daniel was piling acorns into a pyramid. "That, and those flamboyán pods made great swords."

The flamboyáns dropped enormous pods each year, crackly and brown, and Papi and Daniel had gathered them and kept them on the terraza, under the patio furniture. It had annoyed Mami; she didn't like them tracking in dirt, and the pods shed and cracked over time. But Daniel and his friends had used the pods gleefully all year long, as everything from swords to boomerangs.

"Dani really loved that," Carolina whispered.

"And now they're the wake upon the sea," Papi replied. He watched Daniel some more, and didn't blink, not once.

"Papi?" Carolina ventured. She struggled to find the right words. "If someone's not using something, is it okay to borrow it? Like, just to use it for a little while?"

"If you ask permission, then of course it's okay."

"But what if you couldn't ask permission?" Carolina pressed. "Then is it okay?"

"Is there something you want to borrow, Caro? From your cousin?" Papi looked perplexed.

"Oh, no, nothing like that. I was just . . . wondering." Carolina turned to her drawing and furiously added pods at the foot of the flamboyán, pressing her pencil so hard that they grew much too dark, almost black.

"HEY!" Daniel screamed. "CARO!" He came running up the steps to the deck.

Carolina jumped. "Did something bite you? A squirrel?" What if Daniel had gotten rabies? Her heart was racing.

"No! My tooth is loose!"

"Your tooth is loose?" Carolina asked. "Daniel, don't shout like that just for a tooth!"

"But this is only my *second* loose tooth! Ben already lost almost *all* of his."

"Let me see." Papi crouched down in front of Daniel.

Daniel wiggled his tongue on the spot. It didn't look very loose.

"It'll be a few days, I think," said Papi.

"I'm going to tell Mami. Maybe she can yank it out!"

"No!" shouted Carolina.

Papi stared.

"I—" Carolina didn't know why it suddenly seemed so important that this tooth stay right where it was. All she knew was that she didn't want Mami yanking out that tooth. "It could hurt. Plus it could bleed and get infected."

Daniel frowned. "I'm still going to tell her. She has to make sure that the Ratoncito Pérez knows where I am. He might not have heard that we moved." He went bounding into the house to tell Mami. Carolina could hear Mami gushing about it, even with the door closed.

Uncle Porter opened the sliding glass door and joined them on the deck. "Cristina will be happy. She's missed having a young kid around."

Carolina wasn't used to hearing people call Tía Cuca by her real name; in Puerto Rico everyone used *Cuca,* her nickname. She hadn't known that Cuca had an entire other life in upstate New York, with a different name even. Carolina followed Daniel back inside and discovered that Uncle Porter was right—Tía Cuca was over the moon.

"We can get down the old tooth fairy doll!" she exclaimed.

Gabriela was lounging on the leather couch in the living room. "Just give him money," she said. "He's not going to be interested in that doll you have, Mom."

Tía Cuca tsked. "Really, Gabriela. You always *loved* my tooth fairy doll."

Gabriela shrugged. "What can I say? I was young and silly."

But Tía Cuca was already heading to the garage, talking to herself about where she had stored the doll.

Carolina followed Tía Cuca into the garage, which she liked, because it wasn't so dead and air-conditioned in there. It was hot, the type of heat that wrapped you up. It would have been like the heat of home, except that this heat smelled like gasoline.

The bins were all labeled, and Carolina noticed one on the left-hand side that read *Fabric*.

"Tía Cuca?"

"Mmmm?"

"Do you think I could use your fabric sometime?" She pointed timidly.

"¡Claro!" Tía Cuca stopped what she was doing and pulled down the fabric bin. "Do you know how to sew? I could teach you! Gabs was never interested, but maybe you'll be. What do you want to make?"

Caro hesitated. "Maybe some curtains?"

"Curtains?" Tía Cuca laughed. "Gabs would have said clothing, I can guarantee you."

"For when we move into our own house," Carolina added quickly.

"That is just the sweetest thing!" Tía Cuca lifted the lid off, and they sifted through the fabric. Carolina's heart sank. The bin was full of scraps, each piece no more than a foot across. Even if Tía Cuca taught her to sew, it would take ages to make a set of curtains. None of the scraps were yellow either.

But Tía Cuca was on a mission. "I'll get down the sewing machine! I can start teaching you later tonight." She put her hands on her hips. "Now, where's that doll?" Tía Cuca moved aside a toolbox. "Here she is! Oh, isn't she lovely, Carolina? I'm glad you're young enough to appreciate these things."

Carolina forced her face into a smile and nodded. The doll was horrible. She had a porcelain head and hands, but her body was covered in layers of peach-colored, glittery skirts. The fabric was meant to look like chiffon, something gauzy and light, but anyone could tell that it was really cheap polyester. The doll had a sparkly wand and tiara that a few years ago might have fascinated Carolina, but now just looked very, very fake.

Tía Cuca carried the doll out to the kitchen and set it on the counter. "Ana, come look! See, there's a pouch for him to leave the tooth and everything! Isn't it darling?"

Mami came in and helped Tía Cuca fan the skirts. "Oh, he'll love it," Mami said. "I sent him upstairs to take a bath, but just wait until he sees it."

Carolina crossed her arms. "What about the Ratoncito Pérez?" she asked. "That's who Daniel's expecting, he said so."

Tía Cuca beamed at her doll. "Oh, I never liked that. It always freaked me out, even when I was a kid. Mice are so horrible, I don't even like *pretending* to have one in our house."

"Shhhh!" Carolina said. "What are you thinking? He'll hear you."

Mami stared at Carolina. "Caro, it doesn't matter. It's a game, remember?"

"Not to him it isn't! Besides, how would a tooth fairy even work? Mice stow things away; it's in their nature. *Real* fairies are light and airy—they couldn't carry a human tooth."

Tía Cuca opened her mouth. "Well, if you really feel that way—"

"She doesn't," Mami cut in. "She's just tired. She's had a long day. Caro, this is why I don't want you having playdates so late after camp. It's too much for you."

"What?" Carolina glared at Mami. "I'm not tired!"

"Carolina, I want you to apologize to your tía Cuca." Mami turned to Cuca. "It's wonderful, it really is, and Daniel's so lucky that you're so thoughtful." She looked back at Carolina expectantly.

"I'm—I'm sorry, Tía Cuca. I didn't mean that we don't appreciate it."

"Oh, that's okay, honey. Don't worry about it."

Mami gave Carolina a curt nod, and Carolina wandered out of the kitchen, knowing she'd been dismissed.

Gabriela had been listening from the couch in the living room. "Way to go, Caro," she said, looking up from her phone. "That doll's like my mom's favorite thing in the world."

"I didn't mean—"

Gabriela interrupted her. "What's that rat thing you were talking about, anyway?"

"It's not a rat, it's a mouse," Carolina explained. "It makes more sense when you think about it—fairies can't carry teeth."

Gabriela snorted. "Because fairies aren't *real*, remember?"

"In Puerto Rico we had a mouse," Carolina insisted. She felt like she had said it a hundred times in the last hour alone.

"My mom never taught me that," Gabriela said. She went back to scrolling. Her perfectly straight teeth shone in the blue light of the screen, but she didn't smile. "My mom never taught me any of that," she repeated, sadly this time. Then she stood up and headed out of the living room. She paused at the foot of the stairs. "Just don't be too hard on my mom with that doll. She made those skirts herself."

"Okay," Carolina promised. She wouldn't be hard on Tía Cuca. She had never meant to insult the doll in the first place—only to say that this was only Daniel's second loose tooth and she wanted the Ratoncito Pérez to come to him. It made her heart ache to think that this move would take away the Ratoncito Pérez along with everything else.

Carolina's bed that night smelled of Tía Cuca, of shampoo and hair dryer. Tía Cuca had been doing laundry constantly since they arrived, and today was no exception. Uncle Porter joked that she barely gave anyone time to sleep on the sheets before washing them.

Caro snuggled down, trying to get comfortable. As she reached for the light, something caught her eye—*yellow.* These sheets were yellow, bright and cheerful, and Tía Cuca had an entire closet full of sheets, enough to change them every few days. *There's always sheets,* Jennifer had said. Carolina turned off the light, and dreamed of elves, dancing in a yellow breeze.

Chapter Six

Rain poured over the farm the next day, and everything— not only the fields but the whole world, the sky and the dairy and the slide on the playground—was wet and getting wetter.

Carolina's camp group huddled around their table talking while Daniel's counselor, Josh, gathered the younger campers to take them to what would be a very wet garden. Carolina watched Daniel and Ben link arms, and it gave her a warm, cozy feeling. Against the gray day outside, the yellow walls of the camp center looked even brighter.

Lydia stopped by the older kids' table. "I'm going to send your group outside to feed the animals; I don't want everyone indoors all day just because of a little rain."

All five girls turned to the window. Rain rolled down the surface of the glass in a cascade. No one could call this a *little* rain.

Lydia shook her head. "All right, all right, it's a lot of rain, I know. But don't you know the poem?"

Lydia didn't wait for them to respond before reciting,

Let the downpour roil and toil!
The worst it can do to me
Is carry some garden soil
A little nearer the sea.

She grinned at them. "That's Robert Frost. Do you all know him? He was a poet who was also a farmer. Paul liked to quote his poetry."

It didn't make sense, Carolina thought, for Lydia to remind her so powerfully of Papi. They were too different, Lydia gray-haired, Papi with his jet-black hair; Lydia from upstate New York, Papi from the Caribbean. But here was Lydia, quoting poetry like Papi, the same grin, the same joy as she recited to them.

"So," Lydia prompted. "Will you go outside and feed the animals?"

Yuan came up beside Lydia. "Come on, it would be a big help."

Alyssa smiled sweetly. "No problem at all," she said in her high-pitched voice.

"Thanks, Alyssa." Yuan clapped her on the back. "You're all champs."

As soon as Yuan and Lydia were out of earshot Alyssa groaned. "I can't believe we have to go out in this. It's like torrential out there!"

Jamie zipped up her rain jacket and pulled the hood over her head. "It won't be that bad, Alyssa. Just put on your poncho."

Alyssa glared at Jamie. "You sound like my parents. I look ridiculous in it, but they still expect me to wear it. And you look ridiculous in that hood; it makes your face look all scrunched up."

Jamie sighed and pulled down the hood.

"Let's just leave all our stuff here and get wet," Gabriela said. "A little rain never hurt anyone."

"Better than wearing our ugly rain gear, that's for sure," Alyssa muttered.

Jennifer unzipped her backpack and pulled out a green poncho. "Suit yourselves. I'm going to be nice and dry with this on, and so's all my stuff. Want one, Carolina?"

Carolina took the extra poncho Jennifer offered her and pulled it on, being careful to cover her backpack. She was carrying precious cargo. Jennifer pulled her braid forward so it wouldn't get caught under her backpack, then slipped on the poncho. It made her look even zanier than usual. Today she had put bright green leaves in her braid, and between the leaves and the poncho billowing over her and her backpack, she looked like some kind of walking shrub.

Alyssa raised her eyebrows. "Interesting choice, Carolina. I'm not sure green is really your color."

"But no one's going to see her except the sheep, so it's fine." Gabriela pulled Alyssa to the door and shot Carolina a dirty look over her shoulder.

Yuan grabbed her whistle. "They're going to get soaked."

The paths had gone from muddy to all mud since that morning. They passed Daniel's group coming in from their outdoor activity. The kids were flinging the mud at one another and shrieking, and Daniel wasn't wearing his poncho. She was going to look like a comparative angel when she got home, Carolina thought.

"Hey, Caro!" Daniel shouted as he passed her. "My tooth is *even looser* today! And Tía Cuca told me that the tooth fairy she has brings *extra* money!" He whooped and zoomed past Ben on his way inside.

Yuan dashed ahead of them into the sheep enclosure. "Let's make this quick. Lydia just asked us to change the water; George is at a meeting this morning, so she thought we could handle it."

"At a meeting with my father," Alyssa said proudly.

Carolina helped Yuan turn the dirty water out of the trough, then jumped back as it splashed onto her sneakers. Alyssa was wearing pink rubber boots, but she didn't volunteer to help. She stayed by the gate with Gabriela and Jamie while Carolina went with Jennifer to get the hose from the other side of the enclosure.

"Remind me who George is again?" Carolina asked quietly.

"That's Lydia's son." Jennifer hauled the hose over her shoulder. "He used to live in Albany, but he's been around the farm a lot since Paul died."

They reached the trough and helped Yuan fill it with

clean water. When it was full, Jennifer straightened up and shook her braid out, scattering water and slick green leaves onto her poncho. "George might be his son, but he's *not* Paul."

"Everyone's just trying to do their part, Jenn," Yuan said, joining their conversation. "No one is Paul, but it's not easy running a farm alone at Lydia's age."

Alyssa made a show of turning off the hose for them. "I think it's sweet that George is helping."

Jennifer shivered. "How come he has a meeting with your dad?"

"Oh, you know, just talking about some new farm business," Alyssa said in her most angelic tone.

Yuan blew her whistle. "Come on, everyone, let's get back inside; it's too rainy."

The others hurried out of the sheep enclosure, but Carolina grabbed Jennifer by the arm. "Yuan, can Jennifer and I stay outside? We want to visit some of the other animals."

Yuan held the gate open. "It's really wet out here."

"Yeah, but we have these great ponchos." Jennifer flapped out her arms. "We'll come inside if it starts to really come down, promise."

"All right, just don't blame me if you catch pneumonia." Yuan shut the gate behind her and waved to the other girls to keep going.

But instead of heading back to the camp center, Gabriela straggled behind. "Where are you two going?"

"Nowhere, we're just going to hang out!" Carolina tried to look cheerful and innocent.

Gabriela crossed her arms. "Come on. I know you're up to something."

"Gabs!" Alyssa was standing by the gate, clutching her elbows for warmth. "Hurry *up*," she whined. "I'm cold."

Gabriela looked back and forth between Jennifer and Carolina. "Fine, don't tell me, then. Just don't expect me to cover for you later."

"Why would we need someone to cover for us?" Carolina asked, but Gabriela was already marching back to Alyssa.

Jennifer high-fived Carolina. "It'll be an hour before anyone misses us; there's free time now anyway. Come on, let's go."

Hiking through the woods in the rain wasn't easy, and Carolina's socks were soaked by the time they reached the cabin. Inside, Carolina took off her shoes and lined them up neatly by the door, then laid her socks out on the floor to dry. "Too bad we don't have a real fire," she said, curling her toes in front of the fireplace.

The yellow bedsheet was unharmed by the rain. As they held it out, Carolina thought for a moment it might make a good rug, instead of curtains.

"It's the perfect color," Jennifer said. "We'll feel like the sun is streaming through the windows."

"Rain or shine."

They had no ruler to measure with, but they used a spool of string that Jennifer had. They cut the string to match the length and width of the window frame, then laid the string on the sheet to use as a cutting guide.

Carolina thought they would have to hem the edges

properly, but Jennifer said to leave the rough edge. Though neither of them was an expert, they knew enough to take Jennifer's figurine-making supplies and sew a row of stitches on the top side of each curtain, making a tunnel for a rod to pass through.

They leaned on the walls of the cabin as they worked, and it was peaceful, to be inside this cozy house while around them the rain came down, kept coming, down, down, down. At one point, a drip started leaking through the roof, hitting the floor and turning the dust and dirt to mud. They would have to find a way to clean the floor soon, and maybe bring a bucket.

What stumped them was the rod. "I could look in my garage tonight," Jennifer said. "It's full of stuff."

But they wanted to hang their curtains today, so they ran the string through the rod tunnel, tied one end to a rusty nail that was stuck in the wall, and held down the other end on the mantel with heavy stones. The curtains came out lopsided, and begged to be hung properly, but they brought undeniable cheer to the cabin.

Jennifer crouched in front of the fireplace. "Now you'll feel right at home," she told the little elf. "Right at home."

"When I was little I was sure elves were real," Carolina said. "Sometimes I'd imagine they lived in the trees in our yard in Puerto Rico."

"I used to think the figurines I made came to life at night, and I talked to them after my parents turned off the lights. They thought I had an imaginary friend."

Amidst the steady drip of the leaking roof, an idea formed in Carolina's mind, growing stronger with each droplet of water, with each streak of mud skidding across the floor.

"Jennifer," she asked, "do you ever make animal figurines? Could you make a mouse?"

Jennifer sat back. "How come?"

Carolina took a deep breath. "My brother, Daniel, is about to lose a tooth."

"I know; he was shouting it to the entire world, remember?"

"Right. Well, the thing is, when I was little we always used to have the Ratoncito Pérez, not the tooth fairy."

"The raton-*what?*"

"The Ratoncito Pérez. He was just like the tooth fairy, except he was a little mouse. Doesn't that make more sense? How would a fairy fly, with a tooth?"

Jennifer dug through her backpack and pulled out her wire, scissors, and, finally, a tuft of white wool roving. "Oh, I don't know. Fairies are magical; don't you think anything they touched would just become weightless?" Jennifer sprang to her feet and danced around the cabin barefoot. "Like this!" She skipped lightly on the balls of her feet, raising her arms like a ballerina.

Carolina snorted and covered her face with her hands. "You're the spitting image of the tooth fairy."

Jennifer laughed and sat back down. "Okay, so what's the problem? Can't this Pérez character come for Daniel's tooth?"

"That's the thing!" Carolina told her all about Tía Cuca's doll.

Jennifer stuck out her tongue. "Yuck. Whatever happened to just leaving teeth under your pillow? That's what I did when I was little. My dad used to make me these little cards from the tooth fairy; I still have some of them."

"I know, but that's the point. We left our teeth at home under the pillow, too, but my mom always told us it was the Ratoncito Pérez. But all Daniel sees now is that doll, so it doesn't matter what we tell him."

"I see the problem." Jennifer snipped the wire, then quickly bent it into a four-legged shape. She reached for the white roving and hunched over her work, her shoulder and long braid blocking it from Carolina's view.

Carolina laid her sketchbook on the floor and stared at her flamboyán tree. There was only one thing missing now that she'd filled in the blossoms with Jennifer's red pen. She'd never liked drawing people, but she picked up her pencil and sketched a figure of a girl.

"Jennifer?"

"Hmmm?"

"How long have you known my cousin?"

Jennifer's braid grazed the floor as she jabbed the white wool with a needle, teasing it into place. "Practically forever," she said. "She's older than me, but there aren't that many kids in Larksville, and we've been coming to camp at Silver Meadows for years. When she lived in this part of town I used to see her around sometimes. Your aunt and uncle were friends with Lydia and Paul."

Carolina drew the girl's hair, making it swing over her face, so the girl would look like she was bending forward. "It feels strange that everyone in Larksville knows her so well. I'm her cousin, but we've only seen each other every couple of summers."

"Until now."

"Yeah. That's right."

"I bet she doesn't like me much," Jennifer said.

"That's not true!" It was an automatic answer, because she hadn't expected Jennifer to say something so bold. She stopped drawing and chewed on the end of her pencil. "She's just—worried."

"About what people will think."

Carolina twirled the pencil between her fingers. "More like what Alyssa will think." She wasn't sure if that made it better.

"People around here usually are worried about what Alyssa will think." Jennifer threaded a sewing needle with bright yellow thread. "It's because Alyssa's dad is a big shot. He built that whole development where your aunt and uncle live." Jennifer tied a knot at one end of the thread. "Plus Alyssa acts like—I don't know, like Little Miss Sugar and Spice Perfect Pants."

Carolina giggled. "What did you call her?"

Jennifer grinned. "I'm just saying. People feel like they have to live up to her."

"I don't." Carolina picked up her pencil again. She hadn't known that until a moment ago, but saying it out loud made her feel powerful.

Jennifer paused, pulling her sewing thread in and out of a piece of yellow fabric. "I wouldn't want to be like Alyssa," she said slowly. "But still. I know what people say about my family."

"What kind of things— What do they say?" Carolina shaded the sky above the tree furiously, abandoning the girl she was drawing to keep her own hands busy.

"People think we're weird. Because my dad's an artist, and not a famous 'gallery in New York' artist. And because we couldn't afford to buy one of those new houses, even if we wanted to—which we don't," Jennifer added defiantly.

Carolina went back to drawing the girl, and now drew a sketchbook, unfolding in the girl's lap. "I don't think you're weird. I love your house. It's better than my aunt and uncle's house; their house always makes me feel like I'm about to mess something up, like I shouldn't breathe too loud. I love your house—and this place," Carolina added.

Jennifer smiled wide, showing Carolina every one of the rubber-band colors on her braces.

They worked for a few minutes, then Jennifer clipped the end of her thread and held out her creation to Carolina. "It's all done."

Carolina drank in the tiny white mouse. The wool was smooth and soft, and there were wire whiskers poking from the mouse's tiny pink nose, and in its paws, the mouse held a yellow star, which Jennifer had sewn with the leftover yellow sheet.

"It's the Ratoncito Pérez," Carolina breathed. This little

mouse stirred something deep inside, where her whispers flowed in Spanish, and she said aloud, "Maravilloso."

"I added the star, to represent magic."

"Of course." Obviously. This mouse could only be magical.

Jennifer dropped the mouse into Carolina's outstretched palms, then leaned back against the wall of the cabin. "Now we just have to wait for that tooth to come out."

Carolina stroked the wool with her forefinger and marveled at how real this mouse felt, how he seemed to be alive. "I love it. Thank you so much, Jennifer."

They wriggled into their damp socks and sneakers before heading down to lunch, but they stuffed their ponchos back into Carolina's now-empty backpack. The rain had stopped.

They were just crossing the stream when a shadow fell over the bridge from the other side, casting the shape of a man, even a giant.

He was so tall that behind him the farm looked cartoon-like. His hands were on his hips, and he was glaring down at them, and to Carolina it seemed as if he were blocking out the sky, filling the world with his boulder-like head and shoulders. "Shouldn't you girls be inside? It's the middle of the camp day!"

"We were just—" Carolina pointed toward the woods, grasping for words, until Jennifer stepped on her foot lightly.

"Sorry, George!" Jennifer said. "Lydia sent us to gather the eggs, and then we decided to check out the stream since we were already so close. The water's risen a lot, see? It's not as dry as it was before."

Carolina and George glanced down at the stream together, and sure enough, the water was rushing along, deeper and faster than before.

George grunted. "Rain will do that, Jennifer. Not so interesting." He shook his head. "Okay then, get going! My mom is probably waiting for you."

"Bye!" Jennifer waved cheerfully, then grabbed Carolina by the wrist and pulled her past George.

"Keep walking," Jennifer muttered to her. "Look casual." As soon as they were a fair distance away, Jennifer exploded, "What a grinch! My dad told me that George hates farming but he's stuck here since Paul died. I wish he would just go back where he came from!"

"Jennifer," Caro asked, "do you think— Are we trespassing? What if Lydia uses that house—"

Jennifer shook her head. "No one's been in there for ages; we'd be able to tell if they had. Besides," she added, "we're making it better. Now it has curtains. And an elf."

Chapter Seven

Carolina carried the little Ratoncito Pérez in her pocket all week, patting it from time to time. She and Jennifer were already planning their next adventure to the cabin. They were going to find flowers for the windowsill. *Curtains and flowers,* Caro thought, *our little house.* All that was missing was a hearth rug and a rocking chair. She'd never had hot tea, but all the same she imagined herself kneeling at the hearth, lifting a boiling kettle, and serving Jennifer in a dainty teacup.

She was only half listening that Friday night while Mami, Papi, and Tía Cuca stood in the kitchen, discussing who should go to a dinner party they'd all been invited to by Alyssa's parents.

"You should come, Ana," Tía Cuca said. "They'd be happy to have you."

Carolina leaned over the counter and propped her chin

in her hands. Mami loved going to parties; she loved getting dressed up for them and choosing her earrings and spritzing on perfume. But Mami was shaking her head.

"I would love to, but Daniel—"

"We'll call a babysitter!"

"I could babysit," Gabriela said.

Carolina glared at her. "He's my little brother; he'd want me to stay with him."

Tía Cuca clapped her hands together. "Girls! Cut it out! It's very nice of you, but either we're calling a babysitter or someone will stay home. Besides, Gabriela, I thought you wanted to see Alyssa?"

"I do, but—"

"Well then, you're coming with us."

Gabriela muttered something about how she was almost in high school, but luckily Tía Cuca didn't hear anything.

"So will you come?" Tía Cuca asked Mami.

Mami shook her head. "I'll stay home with Daniel. Maybe Gonzalo will go."

"You really should!" Tía Cuca turned to Papi. "Lance has always been very good to us, more than just a boss, really. He may want to follow up after meeting you, he has so many connections—"

"That's not why I want him to go." Mami frowned. "I just think he needs a night out."

"Oh—of course—that's not—"

There was a long and stiff silence, as if Tía Cuca and Mami had misplaced their usual selves, along with their smiles.

"I would love to go," Papi cut in, plastering a bright smile on his face. "It sounds like fun. Okay, Cristina?"

"Yes. Great. Thank you. I mean—" Tía Cuca shook her head, and went to get Uncle Porter upstairs, as if she hoped that he maybe had her lost enthusiasm, and could give it back to her.

Carolina stayed home with Mami, and after they tucked Daniel into bed, Mami settled onto the couch next to Carolina. "What did you do at camp today?" she asked.

"Oh—not much. We went out for a little while, but it was so rainy."

"Are you still playing with Jennifer?"

"Maybe we could read something together?" Carolina asked, dodging the question. Mami had always read to her and Daniel, every night, until a few weeks ago when she'd gotten so busy with the move there hadn't been time for anything. "Gabriela's old books are in the garage." She got up and headed toward the garage.

"Caro," Mami said from the kitchen threshold. "You used to tell me what you were up to."

Caro stopped with her hand on the garage door. She could see herself, in her old school uniform on the terraza of their house in Puerto Rico, telling Mami every detail of her day, telling Mami the stories she made up in her head about fairies and elves, and repeating every bit of instruction Señora Rivón gave her—how it was important to loosen her arm, how she'd studied the ins and outs of the color wheel. "That was then," she said softly, and, *That was when you wanted to listen,* she thought.

She let go of the doorknob, and her arm swung to her side.

"Do you still want to read with me?" Mami asked uncertainly.

Carolina nodded, swallowing hard. "Yes."

In the garage, they ran their fingers over the spines of Gabriela's barely creased books.

"We found a buyer for the house." Mami pulled a book off the shelf and flipped through the pages. A puff of dust rose into the air. "The Realtor called today to tell me someone wants it for the land."

Carolina's throat was tight, and she swallowed with difficulty. "You did?"

"It's such a relief. I have to call Conchita and tell her she can take her Saint Joseph out of the ground," Mami said with a laugh.

Now Carolina wished she had protested, pulled Saint Joseph out when no one was looking, or buried him rightside up. Cousin Conchita's magic had worked, and that was terrible.

"Hang on a second," Carolina said slowly. "If they wanted it for the land, does that mean . . ." In her mind's eye she saw the gate with the padlock, and the blue-and-white tiles of the terraza, and the goldfish in the fountain, the goldfish that had been left alone to die.

"They're going to tear down the old house, of course."

"*What?* They can't do that! It's *our* house—"

"Caro! I was afraid you would take it this way!" Mami

set the book down on the garage shelf. "We had to sell that house, and we're lucky we were able to. What did you expect Papi and me to do, keep a house that no one was living in forever?"

"But what about the yard? What about my bench and all the paths that Papi built?"

"You're being too sensitive, Caro. It's a house. Think about your grandparents. Do you think they sat around and cried about houses when they left Cuba? No. They always said that we were lucky to be together in Puerto Rico, that home is where your family is." Mami cleared her throat. "Tía Cuca and I were apart for a very long time after she left Puerto Rico," she added. "It's good that we're all together now. You should be happy."

The way she said it, Carolina knew it was no use telling her that she *wasn't* happy.

Mami wriggled a book loose from the shelf. She held it out to Carolina. "*Esperanza Rising*. It was your favorite book for years. Do you want to read it?"

Carolina snatched the book and cradled it to herself, then flipped the light to the garage and headed to the living room. She left Mami to find her own way out of the dark garage.

"I remember reading it to you over and over again," Mami called, following Carolina into the living room. "When you were only Dani's age."

Carolina examined the cover, which had a picture of a girl soaring into the sky. She stared at the title, each word capitalized: *Esperanza Rising,* capital, capital, like two staccato notes. At home, she'd had the Spanish edition, where only the first word of the title was capitalized: *Esperanza renace,* the second word falling gracefully after the first, like water rolling down a hill. She could remember that edition perfectly, and she knew exactly which pages were dog-eared, or sticky. She didn't remember packing it, and she wondered where it had ended up.

"Okay, let's read it, then," Carolina said. She didn't meet Mami's eyes, but she settled down on the couch and opened the book. The spine creaked—it didn't look like Gabriela had ever read it.

It was a little strange, reading a book she knew so well in a different language. They'd read other books in English, *Harry Potter* over and over again, but in the world of their old, now-sold house, Esperanza's story had always been told in Spanish.

Mami took the book and put an arm around her. Caro kept her arms crossed while Mami read, and listened to the rhythm of the words, and to the story of the girl. She was surprised to find that it still meant something, that Esperanza was still her, a girl who loved the land, in any language. Esperanza lived on a beautiful ranch in Mexico, but when her father was killed by bandits and her evil uncles set fire to her house, Esperanza and her mother had to flee to California.

At the end of that chapter, Caro said with unintended tears, "We're like them. They lost their ranch, and now we lost our house."

"Ay, Caro," Mami said dismissively. "Hazme el favor. Don't you think you're being a little dramatic? We're healthy. Our family is together."

"I'm happy we're together," Caro said slowly, wishing she could explain it, make Mami see why it mattered so much. The house, the yard, the flamboyán—those had been hers and Mami's, that was where their family had been closest. That was where she had told Mami everything she didn't tell her now.

"We're lucky, Caro. We're so lucky," Mami insisted.

"We're not lucky. You keep saying that, but we had to move and that wasn't lucky, and now you want to be just like everyone else, whatever it takes to be like Cuca and *Gabs.*" Caro spat the nickname out. "You want to do everything just like them."

"Mi cielo, that's not true. I'm just trying—"

"Don't try and deny it! Look what you did with the tooth fairy, you *let* Tía Cuca change everything just like that!" Carolina balled her fists, digging her nails into the palms of her hands.

"Caro, I was being polite. I'm trying to fit in and make things work for us here, I don't know why that's so hard for you to understand," Mami snapped.

The front door flew open, and the alarm system beeped in the hall. Someone typed the code in quickly.

Mami and Carolina stared at each other. Mami's face was white.

"Cristina?" Mami called.

Carolina gripped Mami's hand, her eyes on the entry of the living room, just feet from the front door.

Gabriela rounded the corner.

"Gabriela!" Mami croaked. "You surprised us!"

Gabriela flung herself on the couch and cried noisily, her back heaving as she sobbed.

"What happened, Gabs?" Mami slid closer to Gabriela on the couch and gingerly patted her back. "Is everything okay? Where are your parents?"

Carolina hung back, baffled. Gabriela was always so laid-back, smooth, and cool as a cucumber. Carolina couldn't imagine what could have sent her into such a tailspin.

"My parents are still at Alyssa's; I ran home." Gabriela sat up. "They were all having a fine old time eating dinner outside, so Alyssa and I went inside to listen to music. Then Alyssa tells me that she asked her parents about the next Chiquifancy tour, and they said that they're worried about what type of influence Chiqui has on her. But they mean me." Gabriela crossed her arms and hunched over.

"Your mom says that Alyssa's family loves you," Mami protested. "I can't imagine they really care what kind of music you listen to, mi amor."

Carolina raised her head. "Mi amor" was what Mami called *her*, her and Daniel. It sounded weird, hearing Mami treat Gabriela lovingly, almost like her own.

"Alyssa's so tiny and perfect, and they think I'm going to mess her up!" Gabriela buried her face in her hands and sobbed.

Mami rubbed Gabriela's back. "Shhhhh," she said to Gabriela. "That's all right." To Carolina she said, "Can you go call Alyssa's house and tell them that Gabriela's here? They're probably worried."

Carolina went to the kitchen and rummaged through the drawer. At last, she found an old class list posted to the side of the refrigerator, and sure enough, Alyssa's phone number was on it.

After she hung up the phone, she went back to the living room and sat quietly next to Mami.

"She said—" Gabriela hiccupped. "She said that her parents were worried because Latinas 'get it' sooner." Gabriela inhaled through her nose, shaking slightly from her crying.

"Get what?" Mami asked.

"Puberty. Boobs!"

Mami laughed. "Oh, come on, that's silly."

"It's true! Have you *seen* Chiquifancy?"

"Gabriela, she's a pop star. You know perfectly well that Latinas come in all shapes and sizes just like everyone else in the world."

"They don't!" Gabriela wailed.

Mami looked blankly at Carolina, as if searching for an answer. "Well, maybe your mom could talk to them, or—"

"*No!* That will make everything worse. We can't make Alyssa's dad mad, you've seen how my mom tiptoes around him."

Carolina tried to imagine a world where Gabriela or her body was threatening or scary, but she couldn't. She thought the Rogans should worry more about what kind of influence *Alyssa* had on *Gabriela,* and she said so aloud. "Alyssa acts sweet, but everyone at camp likes you better, Gabriela. They know Alyssa can be slimy behind their backs."

"Well, this is all your fault, Caro!"

"What?"

"It is," Gabriela went on. "It's because you ignore Alyssa, and then you do whatever Jennifer is up to, even if it's something totally annoying like hanging out with the sheep in the pouring rain!"

"We weren't bothering anyone."

"You bothered Alyssa! She had to wait while I talked to you and she wanted to go inside, and anyway it was *weird.* Alyssa hates that stuff—"

"Well," Mami interrupted, "I'm sure Caro can make more of an effort to get along with Alyssa if you think it would help. Won't you, Caro?"

"Yeah, Alyssa's parents would love that. Another Chiqui-fancy to corrupt their daughter." Caro grabbed the book and headed toward the stairs, shaking her head.

"I don't think that's what they meant," Mami called after her, but Carolina knew it was exactly what they meant, and Gabriela knew it too.

Chapter Eight

Carolina paused on her way to the bathroom at the end of the hall. Mingled with the sound of the television downstairs, she heard crying—muffled, sniffling tears.

She stopped and listened outside of Gabriela's door, which was slightly open. Had Gabriela been crying all night? Did Gabriela really blame her for Alyssa's parents? Carolina shook her head. It didn't matter. When she thought of what Alyssa's parents had said, she got so angry, and Gabriela was her cousin. She pushed open the door.

Gabriela didn't move. Her face was buried in a pillow, and the comforter had been kicked to the floor. Carolina tiptoed over and lifted the comforter. "Did you want this?" she asked awkwardly.

Gabriela rolled over. Her nose was red and her face was wet. She took the comforter without saying a word.

Carolina watched Gabriela burrow into the blanket, making a sort of cocoon for herself. "Gabriela?" Carolina asked finally. "Why do you care so much about being friends with Alyssa anyway? She can be so awful."

"You don't know her. She's been my best friend my entire life."

"Then why would she care what I do? Or what her parents think? I don't think *she* has a problem with Chiquifancy."

Gabriela stared at the ceiling. "But her parents are so strict, and if they decide I'm a bad influence . . ."

Carolina shook her head. "Alyssa's parents don't know anything. My mom is right—Puerto Ricans come in all shapes and sizes, and besides, what you look like has nothing to do with how nice you are. You're more angelic than *Alyssa,* that's for sure."

"I guess. Alyssa's no angel, but she's nice to *me.*" Gabriela sank down deeper below the comforter. After a while, she said, "I'm not coming down to breakfast," and rolled over, turning her back to Carolina.

Downstairs, Tía Cuca had set up the sewing machine on the kitchen table. She obviously didn't know Gabriela had been crying, because as soon as she saw Carolina, she said brightly, "I thought we could get started on your sewing lessons! We'll make curtains, like you wanted."

"Oh," Carolina said. "Right." She had forgotten about the sewing lessons, and she wasn't about to tell Tía Cuca why she didn't need to make curtains anymore. While Daniel watched cartoons, Mami read a book, and everyone else slept, Carolina sat next to Tía Cuca and learned to use the machine.

Sewing wasn't bad. At first, the whole thing felt rumbly, like a bumpy train ride, or a boat on choppy seas. But soon, Carolina caught a rhythm, and when she sewed a long seam, there was a glide to it, a flow that Carolina felt when her painting was going well.

Tía Cuca taught her how to line up the scraps, right sides together, piecing together a fabric large enough for curtains. The patchwork had a busy, cozy look, and Tía Cuca told her stories as they sewed each piece: the scrap with the tiny purple-and-white flowers had been a dress for Gabriela, and the seersucker had been a bench cushion. Tía Cuca said it had been a bad choice, dingy after only a few washes.

"Caro," Mami said when Tía Cuca went to put away the sewing machine, "maybe you could do something with your cousin today. She had such a hard night, I'm sure she'd love to play a game with you."

Carolina wondered if Mami knew just how hard the night had been for Gabriela, if Mami, too, had heard Gabriela crying in her room.

"It would be a nice gesture," Mami added.

"I'll ask her when I see her," Carolina agreed.

By the time Gabriela came downstairs, everyone was busy getting ready for the day. The coffeepot was gurgling cheerfully, and Mami was fixing breakfast. When the phone rang, Uncle Porter picked it up. He talked for a moment, then held his hand over the mouthpiece.

"It's for you, Carolina."

Carolina walked over slowly, dragging her fingers along the counter as she went. She took the phone from Uncle Porter and perched on one of the high kitchen stools. "Hello?"

Jennifer sounded like she'd been up since dawn. "Sun's out, do you have a water bottle? Want me to fill one up for you?"

Carolina fiddled with the pad of paper her aunt and uncle kept by the phone, and clicked the top of the pen open and shut.

"Carolina? Are you there?"

"Yeah, I'm here." She looked over at Mami, who was whisking eggs. Carolina loved watching Mami cook: she did it always the same, cradling the bowl in one hand, craning her neck to the side. She did it enthusiastically, like she did everything, like she was trying to conquer the scrambled eggs. But right now, the thought of eggs made Carolina sick.

"I'm supposed to hang out with my cousin," she said softly.

"What? I thought we were going to work on the cabin!"

It was a clear, bright Saturday. There would be fresh air and white light, and Jennifer's mom was working—they could have all day at the cabin without anyone ever finding out.

"Well—let me just ask my mom. I'll call you back."

Carolina set the phone down and asked Mami.

Mami looked up from her eggs. Wisps of hair had come

loose from her ponytail. "Well, I guess it is a Saturday—maybe Gabriela wants to go?" Mami seemed to have decided that if Caro had to have weird friends, maybe she could at least get Gabriela to be weird with them.

Gabriela rolled her eyes and grabbed a bunch of berries off the table. "That's okay, Tía Ana. I'm hanging out here today."

Uncle Porter closed his newspaper. "I thought I was taking you and Alyssa and Jamie to the mall today, Gabs. You must have reminded me three times this week."

Gabriela popped a raspberry into her mouth. "Nope. Not going," she said with her mouth full.

Mami looked worriedly between Gabriela and Carolina. "Caro, if your cousin is staying home, maybe you should keep each other company—"

Gabriela slid off the kitchen stool. "Don't worry about me, Tía Ana, I'll be in my room. Carolina can do what she wants."

Mami sighed. "All right then, Caro, just— What do you even *do* over there, anyway?"

Carolina shrugged. "We hang out. We explore the woods behind Jennifer's house."

"Is that safe, Caro? What does Jennifer's mom think about that?"

"I mean, I'm sure she'd rather we stayed in and read or something—"

Uncle Porter laughed loudly. "This is the country, Ana, kids play in the woods." He folded his newspaper and grabbed the keys off the counter. "Come on, Caro, I'll give you a ride over there; I have to run some errands anyway."

She turned back to Mami. "Can I go, then?"

"Okay," Mami agreed finally.

Uncle Porter winked and headed for the car.

"I've always loved this part of Larksville," Uncle Porter said. They passed a cornfield set close to the road, and the stalks were full and green. "We had some good memories here, Gabs and Cristina and I."

"Then why did you move?" Caro asked.

Uncle Porter considered. "The old house needed more care than we could give it. The roof needed fixing, and it's hard to cook in a very old kitchen like we used to have. Our new house is easier. More comfortable. Besides"—Uncle Porter smiled at her through the rearview mirror—"our new house has space for our family."

Carolina hadn't thought about it that way before, and it gave her a prickly anxious feeling. What would have happened if Uncle Porter and Tía Cuca hadn't had a place for them to stay? Suddenly she was nauseous. *When you're new, you care a lot about your family,* Mami had said.

"All the same," Uncle Porter went on, "it's nice to come out this way and see all the farmland—but don't tell Lance Rogan I said that."

"Because he wants to build new houses here?" Carolina asked.

"Exactly why. A lot of people want the houses, too—there are some new businesses in the area, and of course everyone who works there needs places to live." Uncle Porter shrugged. He dialed off the air conditioner and pushed the switch to roll down the window. "There's a local conservation organization that's been buying up rights to farmland around here. Lance says it's bad for business."

But he breathed in the air from the window, fresh and sweet, and Carolina wondered if he really minded.

Uncle Porter stopped the car in front of Jennifer's house. "I'm glad you've made a friend, Caro. They're good people."

"Can you tell my mom that?" Carolina blurted out.

Uncle Porter guffawed. "She's just a worrywart. She'll come around. Look at Cristina and Gabriela. If your tía Cuca can get used to a daughter as messy as Gabs, your mom can deal with your friends." He motioned to the door. "Hop out and enjoy your day."

Carolina grinned, and she ran all the way to the front door.

Chapter Nine

Weeds poked out of the cracked concrete of Jennifer's driveway. Jennifer yanked the garage door by the handle, and it rolled open with a groan.

"Let's see what we can find." Jennifer dusted off her hands, and Carolina followed her in. The garage was crammed with stuff. Gray sunlight filtered in through the rectangular windows near the roof and made Carolina think of the castle in *Sleeping Beauty,* just as the spell was being lifted and everything was awakening.

They poked around, searching cardboard boxes, slightly damp, for things they could use in the cabin, especially a curtain rod. Carolina kept hoping for a tea set, but after thirty minutes, all they had found were some slightly rusty hooks, which Jennifer said they could use to balance the string they had been using to hold up the curtains.

Carolina fanned herself. She was sweating, and the dust

stuck to her skin every time they moved a box. They cleared a narrow path by stacking boxes on top of one another, then walked sideways, making themselves as small as possible, to the back of the garage.

There were two chairs back there, metal porch chairs with a design of crawling vines on the armrests. They badly needed a new coat of paint, yet they reminded Carolina of the furniture on the terraza in Puerto Rico, with their grated-metal seat bottoms. Even the whinnying noise they made when Carolina tried to lift one up was the same.

Finally, way in the back of the garage, underneath a faded kite, they found scrapers, brushes, and a stack of cans: house paint. Carolina's heart beat fast as they sorted through them. One of the cans had been opened, and dry white paint was caked around the seal. The rest were pristine, completely unused.

"I remember these," Jennifer said. "My dad was thinking of painting the house white, with mint-green trim."

Through the rectangular window, Carolina squinted at the little bit of Jennifer's house she could see. As Mami had pointed out, the paint was flaking off, leaving the house with a pockmarked surface.

"I guess we can't use it, then."

"Don't be silly." Jennifer heaved up one of the heavy cans. "I was five then."

Carolina pushed open the door of the cabin. "We'll have to clean up in here too," she called over her shoulder. She dropped two paint cans and a canvas bag full of trays and rollers on the tiles outside the cabin, and Jennifer took one of the metal chairs inside.

They started with the outside walls in the front, taking the old paint off with a scraper in long, thin curls. Next, Jennifer pried open a can of paint with a screwdriver, and the strong chemical smell mixed with the earthy scent of the forest. It wasn't like an art studio, not like Señora Rivón's, or like Gavin's. Instead it reminded Carolina somehow of Mami, rubbing her nail polish off with acetone and slicking on a new color. But the feeling of painting was similar, and after weeks of sketching in her small drawing pad, Carolina let her arm fly across the door, swishing the minty-green paint back and forth.

They did as much as they could, balancing on the chair to paint the tallest parts of the little cabin. When their backs ached and their paint ran low, they went inside and surveyed their abode.

"It'd be better if that window wasn't broken," Jennifer said, pointing to the left-hand window, the one covered by the tarp.

"I kind of like it." The window glowed greenish blue, as the sun shone through first the blue tarp, then the yellow curtains. "It's almost like stained glass."

"When we hang those curtains properly, and bring up the other chairs, it'll be like a real clubhouse."

"More like an artists' house," Carolina said. "After all, we use it for art." Carolina leaned back against the wall. "Hey, Jenn . . ."

Jennifer beamed at her. "You called me Jenn."

"Is that okay? I heard your dad, the other day."

"Of course it's okay! Can I call you Caro? I heard your cousin call you that, but I didn't know that was a nickname; I'd never heard it before."

Carolina laughed. "Really? There were two Caros in my grade in Puerto Rico."

"But here in Larksville you're the one and only super-special"—Jennifer extended her hand in a sort of bow—"Caro!"

Carolina hugged her sketchbook close to her. "I could get used to that." She turned her sketchbook toward Jennifer, showing her the drawing of the flamboyán tree.

"Whoa, what kind of tree is that?" Jennifer snatched the sketchbook.

"It's a kind that grows in Puerto Rico—and in Cuba, which is where my grandparents are from. My dad told me that every person in his family has had a flamboyán, no matter where they lived."

"They sure don't grow around here," Jennifer said, examining the drawing carefully.

"Do you think—when I get canvas and paints and all—maybe I could make a painting to hang in here?"

"If you made a painting of the tree for the cabin, then there would be a flamboyán here too." Jennifer set down the sketchbook. "Would that make it almost like a home?"

Carolina breathed in the scent of paint and pine needles, of leaves decaying, and in her imagination the trees of this forest stretched out their tall trunks and long branches, to where they reached the flamboyán tree at home, and their dark greens and browns mingled with the flame-red blossoms.

"Yes," Carolina said, "I think that would make it a home."

While the paint dried, they searched the woods near the cabin for a thin, straight stick, one they could use in place of a curtain rod. It was proving nearly impossible to find. Every stick they picked up seemed to be too bendy, or else thick and knobby. They wandered around, searching farther and farther from the cabin, and Carolina started to worry about getting lost, but just then they stumbled upon what seemed to be a treasure trove of sticks, as if they had been broken off and trimmed expressly for Caro and Jenn.

Carolina was just picking up one of the perfect sticks when Jenn put a hand out and stopped her in her tracks.

"What is it?" Carolina followed Jenn's gaze to a ruin of a stone wall, a stretch of piled rocks only a few feet across. A ripped piece of yellow police tape was stuck between the rocks, and it flapped back and forth: CAUTION CAUTION CAUTION.

They inched toward the wall holding hands, and Caro realized that once, not recently, but maybe a century ago, or maybe when the forest had belonged to the fairies and elves, the wall must have marked some kind of path, or the edge of someone's land.

They came close enough to see beyond the wall, where the land fell away steeply and a stream ran through the bottom of a ravine. Perhaps it was the same stream that cut across the foot of Cooke's Hill, or maybe another one altogether. They stared down at it, and went no farther.

"This is it," Jenn said. "This is where Paul fell. I can feel it."

Carolina could feel it, too, the way the wind here slinked around, slapping the police tape and rushing by them, as if it had something to be guilty about.

"We're not supposed to go off of the trail," Jenn said, repeating the words as if she'd never heard them before. "Because of this. Because of Paul."

They moved more quickly through the woods on their way back to Jennifer's house. Carolina didn't worry about getting lost anymore: she was starting to recognize individual trees, their knobby spots and the particular twists of their branches. The ribbons Jennifer had tied easily marked the way down the hill. It was a little cumbersome carrying the empty paint cans, but the cabin was so small, and they wanted space for their art supplies. They tucked away the paint cans in the garage and headed inside.

Jennifer's mom was in the kitchen drinking coffee. "You must be Carolina! I'm Fiona. Have a seat. I'll make you kids some sandwiches." She started spreading peanut butter on toast. "Jenn, what are you working on? You have white paint all over you."

Jennifer turned beet red. "You know. The same thing as always."

Fiona sighed. "You're not onto those elves again, are you, Jenn? You're practically a teenager, honey." She pulled the jelly out of the refrigerator. "What are your interests, Carolina?" She said it hopefully, like maybe the answer would be "algebra."

"Carolina's a painter, like Daddy."

"That's not true," Carolina said quickly. "I just like to paint."

"Now that's the kind of art a young woman should be interested in. What do you like to paint? Landscapes or figures? Or abstract?"

"L-landscapes," Carolina stammered.

"My favorite!" Fiona exclaimed. "That's why I fell in love with Jenn's dad. He kept painting me these landscapes—first it was the ocean, then it was farms: green pastures and red barns, and before I knew it I was packing my bags and moving out to the country with him. A *landscape* artist." Fiona propped her chin in her hand and looked at Carolina in a way that made her a little uncomfortable, and also bubbly inside, like she'd just heard some unexpected and wonderful news.

Caro took a bite of the sandwich that Fiona had made for her, and set it down on her plate. She liked how everyone was eating however they wanted; Fiona was leaning over the counter, and Jenn was perched on a kitchen stool. "I think Jenn's elves are cool. I wish I could do something like that, but I only know how to paint."

"You keep doing your painting. And show Jenn's dad

your paintings next time you see him. He loves talking to other painters."

Carolina didn't bother to tell Fiona that they weren't paintings, that she hadn't done anything but draw in her sketchbook for weeks and weeks. Instead she shoved the rest of the peanut butter and jelly sandwich into her mouth, and washed it down with a big gulp of milk. "Okay."

Jennifer patted Carolina on the back. "Don't choke on that sandwich, Caro, my mom will never forgive herself." She leaned forward, her braid swinging in front of Caro's face, and whispered, "You should show my dad, though. Then you can get to work on the painting—for our cabin."

After Fiona left for her afternoon shift, the house was quiet, and the girls stayed inside for a while, enjoying the empty space and the dusty sunlight, how cool and still it felt.

"There's a stand down the road that sells flowers," Jennifer said after a while. We could go get some."

"Or we could clean," Caro said. "The cabin needs it."

"If you put it that way, then I *definitely* want to go buy flowers. Come on, let's go now."

They turned off of Jennifer's street and walked on the main road. After the shade of the forest, the sun made Carolina feel bare and exposed. She felt like an ant, crawling single file along an endless stretch of blacktop. The dashes of yellow paint were new, starkly marking the way to Larksville, and the new houses just beyond.

Jennifer tented both hands over her forehead to shade her eyes. There was a smell of hot rubber and new blacktop.

"My mom worries a lot," she said suddenly. "She thinks I'll get made fun of at school if I talk about elves, and when I walk on this road she gets nervous. She thinks I'll get hit by a car just because there's more traffic now." Jennifer kicked a loose bit of asphalt. "But I used to walk on this road all the time before they built all those new houses."

Carolina edged a little more to the side of the road, closer to where the weeds and the grass grew. "Moms are different with their own kids," she said, and as soon as she said it she knew it was true. "It's like how for my mom, Gabriela always does everything right, and no matter what she does, it's what my mom says I should do."

"Why?" Jenn threw her arms up, in general frustration at moms.

Caro shrugged. "Gabriela's the right—" She was about to say "the right amount of Puerto Rican," but she corrected herself. "She's Puerto Rican in the right ways, and my mom likes that."

Jenn stopped walking. "You never talk about it. About Puerto Rico."

It surprised Carolina, and she couldn't respond. She thought about Puerto Rico all the time, thought about it in the cabin and in the woods, and every breeze, every droplet of water was measured against home. But she hadn't told Jennifer about any of that; she'd kept the thoughts close to her heart and hadn't said a word. She didn't know what was stopping her.

"Well," Jennifer added, "you talk about the trees. The flamboyán trees, with the red blossoms."

Carolina almost laughed, but then she paused. "That's because I'm Puerto Rican, or Cuban, or whatever I am, in that way: I like the trees, and the yards. It's the colors, really. I like how the air felt at home, and how the ocean smelled." Caro shook her head. "But Gabriela can dance the Fancy, and I can't."

"And even if the music is awful," Jenn finished for her, "my mom would still be thrilled if I were suddenly into Chiquifancy. Almost-middle-schoolers are *supposed* to like Chiquifancy. We're not supposed to like elves."

Carolina agreed almost wholeheartedly, except she didn't think Chiquifancy's music was terrible. She liked the music, loved how Chiqui wove in so many different styles, rhythm blending with the Cuban flute, high and sweet. Carolina thought Chiqui's music was joyous and true, but she couldn't imagine dancing like that, moving her feet or her hips like Gabriela did, wearing her hair long down her back or up in a side sweep. No wonder Mami sometimes thought she was strange, to be Puerto Rican and Cuban all rolled into one and still too shy to dance the Fancy.

They reached the farmstand on the side of the road. The ground sloped down behind it, and there was a little house tucked away amidst the trees. While Jennifer and Carolina considered the flowers in black plastic containers, a screen door creaked open, and two women came out carrying cardboard boxes piled with vegetables.

"Lizbeth, you know we don't have that kind of money," said one of the women. "There's no way we can compete with the developers around here."

Carolina looked up from the stand. The woman who had spoken had short hair and skin a little darker than Mami's.

"Still," Lizbeth sighed, "if we had our own farm, we could start projects—big ones—and it would be ours, really ours, Alicia. We've been saving so long." She balanced the box on one hip and flipped her ponytail over her shoulder. Her hair was wavy and golden, almost as long as Jennifer's.

Alicia shook her head. "I think we're going to be saving a lot longer."

"We could do it now," Lizbeth said confidently. "If one of the conservation organizations—" She stopped as they approached the farmstand. "Hi there!" she said to Jennifer and Carolina. She smiled, and the freckles on her cheekbones lifted up.

"Do you have everything you need?" Alicia asked. "Need any help?"

Carolina held up the flowers she had picked up, and noted the price sign taped to the side of the stand. She and Jennifer pulled their money out of their pockets and added up the total. Between them both, they had a little extra. Carolina knew she didn't need to ask Jennifer before handing all the bills to Alicia.

Lizbeth started to count out change, but Carolina shook her head. "Couldn't you keep it?" she asked shyly.

"She means for the farm," Jennifer added. "I know farms cost a lot, but—" She shrugged.

Lizbeth put her hand to her heart. "That's so sweet."

Alicia grinned. "We can't do that, you're kids!" Carolina

noticed now that she wore a tiny sparkling nose ring. "I'll tell you what," Alicia said. "Take these too." She handed Jennifer a set of small white flowers. "They'll look nice together."

They waved good-bye, and Carolina and Jennifer headed back down the road, admiring their colorful flowers as they walked.

After a while, Carolina cleared her throat. "Señora Rivón—she was my art teacher—used to tell me that you always have to paint things like they really are, not like you think they should be. She said most of the time we don't see things right, because we only see what we already think is there." Carolina noticed now that there were cars zooming past them. "Maybe your mom just hasn't seen you yet, not really."

Jennifer walked ahead of Carolina, her chin resolute, perfectly parallel to the smooth blacktop. As they turned onto the back road that plunged into the woods, she said, "I'm not going to be who she wants to see. I'm going to be someone who makes elves even if I'm a million years old." They paused on the soft gray gravel beneath the shady trees. Jennifer put her hands on her hips. "And that's final."

Chapter Ten

Daniel was under the big oak tree, poking the grass with a stick. There was something clenched tightly in his fist.

"Whatcha doing?" Carolina sat down beside him while Mami locked the car door.

"Nothing." He opened his hand wide. "Just looking at my collection. Ben and I have been collecting cool things." In his palm was a tiny pinecone, a twist of green twine from a hay bale, and a downy chicken feather.

"What are you going to do with the collection?"

Daniel stroked the chicken feather. "It could be a little blanket, for someone tiny."

"Like an elf?"

"It'd be perfect for an elf."

"I bet the elves could find something useful to do with the twine too."

Mami interrupted. "Are you kids being silly again?"

Carolina looked up at Mami, into her brown eyes, lighter and more muted than Carolina's own. The sun brought out highlights of red in Mami's dark brown hair, and a tiny bit of sparkling silver. Carolina hadn't realized that Mami had stopped dyeing her hair, not until she saw that bit of gray. "I don't think it's silly, Mami. I think it's cool."

She turned back to Daniel, conscious of Mami walking past them, leaving them outside as she headed into the house.

Daniel beamed up at Carolina. He stuffed his collection back in his pocket and gave her a big thumbs-up. "I think *you're* cool," he said.

"Wait a second!" Carolina grabbed Daniel by the shoulder. "Your tooth came out!"

Daniel spread his mouth wide with his fingers. "It happened this afternoon! It was *really* bloody."

"Ewww."

Daniel raced to the door. "Mami had to wash it off and put it in a ziplock baggie, but then Tía Cuca left it for the tooth fairy already! Come look!"

Daniel dragged Carolina to the kitchen counter, where the tooth fairy doll was standing. He scrambled up a stool and held open the pouch so Carolina could see his tooth, wrapped in a plastic baggie, inside. He patted the fairy's skirts. "I know you're going to bring me something good."

"I bet she will!" Tía Cuca said from the stove, where she was making dinner.

"I'm going to see what Papi's doing," Daniel said, dashing out of the kitchen.

"Carolina, can you go check on Gabriela?" Tía Cuca asked. "She's been in her bedroom all day."

"I'm right here, Mom." Gabriela shuffled into the kitchen wearing her sweatpants, her hair in a messy bun.

"Honey, you need to get outside tomorrow. All this moping—"

"I'm fine," said Gabriela. "Let's just eat."

Tía Cuca looked at Caro, as if to say, *Do something.*

"We'll go get everyone," Caro said quickly.

"They're all still upstairs," Tía Cuca complained, balancing a roasting pan with one hand. "But dinner's ready now."

In the stairwell, Gabriela shook her head. "She won't stop asking me *questions.*"

"My mom's the same way," Caro said. "I guess it comes with being sisters." She paused at the top of the steps. "Look, Gabriela. I'm sorry about Alyssa. I'm sorry I wasn't better at making friends with her."

Gabriela lightly kicked the banister. "I didn't mean what I said. It wasn't your fault." Then she went on in a biting, bitter tone, "Not that it matters *whose* fault it is if Alyssa and I can't be friends anymore."

Awkwardly, Carolina patted Gabriela's back. Gabriela stood there for a second, looking small and rumpled, before she shrugged off Carolina and climbed up the last few steps. "Dinner's ready!" she shouted in the hall.

While they ate, Carolina wondered what Daniel would get from the tooth fairy. At home, Mami and Papi had always left a dollar. But it was Tía Cuca's fairy doll, and maybe she would want to add something this time. Carolina wanted Daniel to get more from the Ratoncito Pérez than the tooth fairy, but not so much that anyone would notice.

She was going to use her birthday money. She'd turned eleven right before they left home, and her aunts and uncles had given her cash because Mami had said that they could not pack or store one single thing more. Having the money had never felt right: only two weeks before her birthday, she'd seen a set of oil paints that strapped neatly into a briefcase for travel, but Mami had shaken her head and said that they were just making do and couldn't afford extras right now. The memory had made the birthday money feel tainted somehow, and Carolina wished her family had given it to Mami and Papi and not to her. She'd been saving the cash, thinking that when Papi had a job in New York she would use it to buy the paints herself, that by then it wouldn't feel wrong anymore, but giving some of it to Daniel would be better. It would assuage the guilt faster.

As soon as they finished dinner, Carolina offered to put Daniel to bed.

"That's so lovely of you to offer," said Mami. "I could come up, too, if you want to read together again—"

"No, that's okay!" Carolina hoped her voice wasn't coming out too high-pitched. "You should take a break, Mami. I'll read to Daniel so you can relax."

Mami had her hands on her knees, ready to get up and come with them. "Wow, I don't know what to say."

Papi put a hand on Mami's shoulder. "Say thank you."

Carolina took Daniel's hand and made a beeline up the stairs before Mami could think too much about it. She got Daniel into his pajamas quickly and made him brush his teeth and splash cold water on his face. When she had him neatly tucked into bed, the comforter pulled right up under his chin, she went back to her room and retrieved the tiny mouse that Jennifer had made.

"This is for you."

Daniel sat up and took the mouse. His jaw was hanging open.

"Do you like it?"

Daniel held his fingers to his nose like whiskers and made kissing noises. "It's a little baby mouse, and I'm a little baby mouse too."

"He's not just any little mouse; he's the Ratoncito Pérez and he's going to bring you another treat for your tooth."

"But I already gave my tooth to that fairy downstairs. I don't have another for him."

"That's okay. He doesn't mind. It's just a nice thing he likes to do for Puerto Rican kids who lose their teeth."

Daniel patted the mouse. "Thanks, Mr. Mousie."

"You have to call him Ratoncito Pérez."

"Okay, Mr. Ratoncito," Daniel went on, "I think you've got to go under the bed. Mice don't sleep in kids' beds, otherwise people get mousetraps. Tía Cuca told me she can't stand mice."

"Good idea." Carolina could hardly believe her luck. This way, she wouldn't have to worry about anyone seeing the little mouse.

All that was left was figuring out what the grown-ups would put in the tooth fairy doll. She had hoped she would see them putting it in the doll's pouch, but they must have done it while Carolina was upstairs with Daniel, because they didn't mention it, and Carolina thought it would seem suspicious or, worse, greedy if she asked.

So she waited until everyone was asleep, then tiptoed down the stairs.

Nighttime at home had been the sound of the coquís and cars, chirping and passing. At home, the steps were concrete, and made no sound.

Here, in between the air-conditioning's cycles, there was silence. The stairs were wood, and they creaked as she walked, and so did the floors. The sounds of the night were pushed out, and the only light was the flashing green of the alarm system.

Carolina made it into the kitchen and reached into the pouch. She held the bill up to the green light to see what it was.

Someone flipped on the kitchen light and Carolina's eyes burned from the glare.

"Stealing from your brother?"

Carolina shrieked and clapped her hand over her mouth. Gabriela was standing there in her pajamas.

Carolina glanced at the five-dollar bill in her hand. "No—it's just—" Why hadn't she thought of an excuse in case she was caught?

Gabriela crossed her arms. "I can't believe you, Carolina. Put it back."

Meekly, Carolina tucked the five-dollar bill back into the tooth fairy's pouch. "It's not what it looks like."

"You mean you didn't just reach into the tooth fairy's pouch and take that money?"

"I wasn't taking it!" Carolina said in an urgent whisper.

"Yeah right," Gabriela hissed back. "I'm telling my parents." She walked away.

Carolina dashed behind Gabriela and grabbed her by the shoulder. "You can't! Please, let me explain."

Gabriela paused at the threshold between the kitchen and the living room. She gave Carolina a withering look and flipped off the lights.

The air-conditioning started again, and beneath its rattle Carolina could take the stairs two at a time without having to worry about the squeaking sound. She burst into Gabriela's room just seconds behind her.

"I'm going back to bed." Gabriela yanked her comforter and climbed under the covers. "You've done enough damage without keeping me up half the night."

Carolina pulled the door shut behind her, climbed over the piles of magazines on the floor, and sat on Gabriela's director chair. "You can go to sleep, but I'm going to talk."

"Fine. I'm not going to listen to you anyway." Gabriela folded her arms and squeezed her eyes shut.

"I wasn't trying to take Daniel's tooth fairy money. I love Daniel. He's my little brother, remember?"

Gabriela's eyelids twitched.

"I wanted to see how much the tooth fairy was giving

Daniel, because I want to leave him something from the Ratoncito Pérez too."

Gabriela opened one eye. "The mouse?"

"Yes, the mouse." Carolina cleared her throat, and now she told Gabriela more—she told her about how the Ratoncito Pérez was fond of taking teeth, and then once she got started she kept going, and told Gabriela the folktale of the Cucarachita Martina, the cockroach who married a mouse. Carolina had always wondered if it was the same mouse or someone else altogether.

"You mean the story doesn't say? Wouldn't it mention if the mouse was running off to collect teeth all the time?"

Carolina shrugged. "In my imagination it was always the same mouse."

"I wish I had learned this stuff when I was little. Like you." Gabriela pulled a loose thread on her comforter, frowning at how it bunched. In the orange glow of the bedside lamp, Gabriela looked gentler: her hair was a little wavy at the ends, and the sweatshirt she slept in was pilled and fuzzy.

"I don't think my parents are going to teach Daniel. But I am." Carolina sat up a little straighter.

Gabriela pursed her lips. "At least you *lived* in Puerto Rico. I don't even speak Spanish."

It was as if Carolina was seeing Gabriela for the first time: not her long legs, or her black hair, or her straight and shiny teeth, but her face, the curiosity and sadness in her eyes. "Well, I could tell you about Puerto Rico, if that's what you want. It's not like you haven't been there."

Gabriela shook her head. "It was such a long time ago, and we were only there for a few days." She kicked off the comforter. "It's totally unfair. The Rogans think I'm some kind of sexy-Chiquifancy-nightmare just because I'm Puerto Rican, and then I don't even know about the Pérez guy! It's a lose-lose-*lose* situation!"

"At least you can dance. I can't."

"A lot of good that does me if I don't have friends."

"I have an idea," Carolina said. "I could show you my sketchbook. I drew lots of stuff from Puerto Rico, and things for Daniel—like the Cucarachita Martina. It's not the same as being there, of course, but if you want to see it—"

"Yeah," Gabriela said. "I'd like that. Sometime." She slouched down and stared into space, as if she were too tired to move.

Carolina tried to think of things that might cheer up Gabriela, pull her out of this desperately sad state. "I like how you're never uncomfortable," she blurted out finally.

Gabriela jerked her head up. "Huh?"

"I mean"—Carolina searched for the words for what she meant—"I always feel awkward. Sometimes when I have an idea or I'm worried about something I can't stop thinking about it, until it all starts going around and around in my brain and everything I say comes out all clunky. I like how you're always—I don't know, graceful. Nothing seems to bother you."

"Lots of things bother me."

"Like us moving here?"

Gabriela stared at her hands. "It's not that you moving here bothers me. I actually kind of like that our house isn't so empty anymore. My parents used to obsess over me all the time; now they can worry about you and Daniel some of the time. It's just . . ."

"I'm weird," Carolina finished for her.

Gabriela shook her head. "No, you're not. Actually, you know what? You're not at all." She swung her legs over the edge of the bed and stood up. "Or if you are, I don't care. I'm done caring." She marched across the room.

"Where are you going?"

"To your room. I want to see your sketchbook." Gabriela took Carolina's hand firmly, yanked open the door, and led her across the hallway of the sleeping house.

They huddled on Carolina's bed together, and Carolina flipped through her sketchbook, searching for a drawing she'd made from a photo of the house her grandmother had lived in. Señora Rivón had told her it was a good drawing because she'd captured the shade of the palm fronds hitting the house perfectly, taking into account the angle of the sun and the shape of the tree.

"This was our grandmother's house," Carolina said proudly. "Mami and Tía Cuca's mom, Carmen. My mom had a photo of the house from before Abuela Carmen died, and I drew it." She went to turn the page, but Gabriela took the sketchbook out of her hands and examined it.

"I remember that house," Gabriela said. "From when we visited when I was little. There was this statue of the

Virgin Mary in the backyard, and a little fountain. There were goldfish in it." Gabriela closed her eyes. "Lots of birds too. There must have been a bird feeder. And wind chimes." She opened her eyes. "I loved that house."

Carolina stared at her and took back the sketchbook. "That's wasn't Abuela Carmen's house. That was my house. The one we're selling." She closed the book.

"Oh." Gabriela eyed the book again. "I'm sorry."

"It's okay." Carolina took a deep breath. "I guess I could tell you about my house too. It was a good house."

Gabriela inched closer to Carolina. "Want to hear a secret? I loved our old house. My parents said it was too small and it was always too hot or too cold because it was so old, but I still didn't really want to move. Even though I have a bigger room and I live closer to Alyssa now—not that that matters anymore—I still miss it."

"I have a drawing of the fountain." Carolina tucked her hair behind her ear and spread the sketchbook across both of their laps. Gabriela's hair smelled like vanilla and coconut, and Carolina wondered if that was what made it so shiny. She showed Gabriela the drawing of the fountain and, finally, the latest drawing she'd made, of the flamboyán tree in the yard. "That was where I used to do my drawing." She wiped her nose with the sleeve of her sweater.

Gabriela examined the flamboyán tree for a long time, saying nothing. Then she said, "We've got to talk our parents into taking us to visit soon."

"Someday," Carolina said, knowing that if it had been

years since Uncle Porter and Tía Cuca had bought three plane tickets to Puerto Rico, it might be even more years, ages, before they went again.

Gabriela handed back the sketchbook, reverently. "Don't you have to bring Daniel his Pérez-guy money? I don't want you to forget."

"The Ratoncito Pérez!" Carolina jumped to her feet and pulled an envelope from her bottom drawer. She took out a ten-dollar bill, put back the envelope, and beckoned to Gabriela to follow. "He sleeps like a rock," Carolina whispered. Together, she and Gabriela tiptoed into Daniel's room, and Carolina slithered under the bed and placed the ten dollars underneath the Ratoncito Pérez.

Carolina shut the door behind her carefully, and she and Gabriela were once more alone in the dark hallway.

"Bedtime, I guess," Gabriela whispered. Then she hugged Carolina, quickly, with a light pat on the back. "Night, cuz."

Chapter Eleven

Daniel shook Carolina awake at dawn. "Look!"

In the half-light, Carolina squinted at the fuzzy white mouse cupped in Daniel's left hand—and the ten-dollar bill clutched in his right. She smiled sleepily.

"Remember to say thank you." Her voice was scratchy; it was so early.

"Gracias, Mr. Ratoncito Pérez."

"Remember, he probably wants it to be kept a secret. Not everyone likes mice."

"Don't worry, Mr. Ratoncito Pérez. I'll keep your secret."

Daniel climbed up onto Carolina's bed with the little mouse. "What are you going to do today, Caro?"

Carolina propped herself up with one elbow. "I don't know. I want to go over to Jennifer's again, but I don't know if I can. Mami might not like it."

Daniel had started making kissy faces at the Ratoncito Pérez. "So?"

"Well, I don't want her to be mad at me."

"Why not?" Daniel kicked his legs from the edge of the bed. "Mami gets mad at me all the time, but she still loves me." He squeezed his eyes shut and beamed his toothless smile at Carolina.

"Who wouldn't?" She reached over and tousled Daniel's hair. Then she patted the mouse figure with her index finger. Maybe Daniel was right, maybe Carolina could do things that Mami didn't like and still be Mami's Carolinita, still be mother and daughter. After all, Daniel was smart for his age.

Downstairs, Mami and Tía Cuca gathered around for Daniel to get his gift from the tooth fairy. Daniel punched the five-dollar bill into the air. "Now I'm *really* rich!"

True to his word, Daniel said nothing about the Ratoncito Pérez. Gabriela, leaning casually against the counter, ate a cup of yogurt. "Way to go, Daniel," she said, then turned to Carolina. "You're going to Jennifer's today, right?"

"Why don't you invite Jennifer over here?" Tía Cuca asked. "I want you to really feel like this is your house, Caro."

Carolina hesitated. It would be nice to have Jennifer over; she was sure that if Mami got to know Jennifer she wouldn't worry as much when Caro was with her. But if Jennifer came to Tía Cuca's, they wouldn't get to go to the cabin.

"She can't," Gabriela filled in. "I was going to invite Jamie over today, remember?"

"It's a big house," Tía Cuca said. "I'm sure there's plenty of room—"

"That's okay," Carolina said quickly. "Jennifer already said her dad would come get me. Next time, Tía Cuca."

Gabriela gave Carolina a knowing smile. Carolina tucked her hair behind her ear. Had Gabriela just stuck up for her?

While Daniel and the grown-ups sat down at the kitchen table, Carolina rummaged for milk in the refrigerator.

"What's Alyssa doing today?" Tía Cuca asked tentatively, and there was a long pause before Gabriela replied.

"I think she's going to the lake. But I didn't want to go."

"This isn't still about the other night, is it, honey?"

"Nope," Gabriela replied.

"Okay, just remember that Alyssa's dad—"

"Is Daddy's boss." Gabriela pushed herself away from the counter and left the kitchen.

The soapy water sloshed around the bucket as Jennifer and Carolina tried to sync their steps. They were spilling all over the place, and over her shoulder Carolina saw trails of water running like hot lava down the dry hill.

"I feel like Jack and Jill," Jennifer complained.

"That's actually one thing I like about Larksville," Carolina said. "I always feel like I'm living in a story."

They reached the cabin and unlatched the door. "This place makes me think of Rumpelstiltskin," Jennifer said, setting the bucket down inside. She lifted the elf out of the fireplace and held him cupped in her hands. The glow of the tarp in the window illuminated her hands, and Carolina could almost see it: Jennifer spinning straw into gold as deftly as she felted and carved and sewed. There was a sparkling ribbon woven through Jenn's braid today, and Caro had thought it was a concession to Fiona, but now she saw it for what it was—a little bit of magic, made of string.

They scrubbed the floor, washing months, maybe years, of dirt away.

"You do know that it's only going to get dirty again?" Jennifer joked, watching Carolina's enthusiastic scrubbing.

Carolina held up her sponge, which was black with dirt. "This dirty?" She squeezed the sponge out in the bucket, and the soapy water quickly turned brown, and soon black.

"It was a joke," Jennifer mumbled.

Realizing how sharp she had sounded, Carolina sat back on her heels. She put down her sponge.

"My parents sold our house in Puerto Rico," she said finally. "The new owners are going to tear the whole thing down." She rubbed her eye, ignoring the soap she smeared across her face. "Before we left, my mom cleaned the whole place. We scrubbed it from top to bottom. She shouldn't have done that, not if they were just going to tear it down."

"Oh," Jennifer said softly. She scooted closer to Carolina. "The house with the flamboyán tree."

They were quiet a long time, long enough to notice the wind chimes and the golden ribbon, how the chair rocked slightly in place, and how it all smelled of earth and paint.

Everything seemed to blend together, home and Jennifer and the cabin and Puerto Rico. The flamboyán tree in Cuba and the one in Puerto Rico were the same tree that grew inside Caro, and now, she realized with a rush, in Jennifer. The bulldozers could knock the world over, but Caro had followed the secret path, and here she was: hidden.

"Right." Carolina straightened up, shaking off the trance. "Let's get this place into shape." She ticked off things that needed to be done: The floor was clean, the curtains hung. The other metal chair needed to be brought up from the garage, and both needed another coat of paint. The house paint was almost done, all but for the trim on the door and window frames. Carolina still wished for some kind of coffee table, maybe a box with a piece of fabric thrown over it, and something real to drink out of: their plastic bottles were all wrong for this elfin place.

"Once it's done—" Caro started.

"We'll throw a fancy ball!"

Carolina raised her eyebrow. "I can't dance, remember?"

"Not for us, silly, for the elves. They can invite the fairies." And Jennifer unloaded more of her figures, turning the fireplace into a tiny village. Carolina could almost hear the little statuettes talking and laughing, and yes, even dancing. She was grateful for their company.

Chapter Twelve

Tía Cuca knocked on Carolina's door. "Hey, sweetheart," she said, letting herself in. "I'm taking Gabs to the mall for a little while. Jamie's birthday is in two weeks and she wants a dress. Do you want to come?"

Carolina was about to reply no, but then she had an idea. "Actually," she said, amazed at how bold her own voice sounded, "I've been thinking of getting something with my birthday money."

Tía Cuca brightened. "I'm so glad! I'll tell Gabs you're coming! It's been hard for her lately—she's always had so many friends, and now this rift with Alyssa . . ."

Caro slipped into her sneakers. "I think Gabs is doing the right thing."

"It's only—well, Gabs always does the right thing— but she and Alyssa were such good friends, since they were babies practically." She sighed. "It'll be good for all of us to get out of the house, at least."

They asked Mami along, and it was odd for once to be with Gabriela and Tía Cuca, where Mami wanted her to be, instead of the one on the outside, knowing Mami wanted her with them. But Mami was delighted that Caro was going; Caro thought Mami's teeth might fall out from smiling so wide. Mami was going to stay home with Daniel and Ben, who were playing in the yard, but said Caro should go. "Can I give you some money, Caro? In case you want to buy something?"

"Oh—that's okay, Mami. I have my birthday money, re-member?"

"Right, of course." Mami put away her wallet, and they all stood around awkwardly, except for Gabriela, who got Tía Cuca's car keys and waved them to the door.

Tía Cuca and Gabriela were interested in clothes, clothes, clothes, which they scrutinized in the dressing room and about which they asked Carolina detailed questions. Caro never knew how to answer. Everything looked fabulous on Gabriela as far as she could tell, but she was clearly supposed to have intelligent thoughts about clothing, so she came up with halfhearted responses—"cute" and "mmm"—and tried cocking her head to the side, to make it look like she was really considering.

But when Gabriela tried on a sparkly fitted dress, Carolina didn't have to pretend. "It's beautiful," she gasped.

Gabriela looked at herself in the mirror and twirled

in place. She smoothed the fabric over her thighs, a smile spreading across her face.

"Gabs, that's perfect for Jamie's birthday party!" Tía Cuca said.

Gabriela's face fell. "No," she said, "it's not." She peeled off the dress, and Tía Cuca and Carolina exchanged confused looks.

"Didn't you like the dress, honey?"

"It's too low-cut."

Tía Cuca wriggled the dress onto its hanger. "You're thirteen, Gabs, you can wear it!"

"No," Gabriela said firmly. "I don't want Alyssa to think . . ." She got busy refolding a pair of jeans, and didn't finish her sentence.

Tía Cuca sighed and hung the dress on the back of the door.

"Wait." Caro took the dress off the hanger and handed it back to Tía Cuca. "You should get it for her anyway. It looked really great."

She had realized suddenly that she did have an opinion about clothing, which was that her cousin was unbelievably gorgeous, and it was both sad and frustrating if Alyssa stood between her and this sparkly, sophisticated dress.

In the mirror's reflection, Carolina watched Gabriela look up, and in her expressive black eyes, Carolina saw hope.

There was no art supply store in the mall. She stood in front of the directory, scanning the names of the businesses over and over again, and Gabriela stood next to her.

"What did you want to get?" Tía Cuca asked.

"Paint," Gabriela answered for her, even though Carolina had never told her what she wanted. "Caro's an artist."

"I didn't know that."

"I just like to draw," Carolina said quickly.

"Hmmm." Tía Cuca studied the directory. "I don't know where there's an art store around here. We may have to look online."

They wandered aimlessly. They stopped at a home goods store, and Tía Cuca bought a set of sheets. "I can't seem to find those yellow ones I had, and I like to have three sets." She paused. "The washer must have eaten them."

Guiltily, Carolina realized the sheets were for her, but Tía Cuca had already bought the replacement set and was leading Gabriela and Caro through the mall again, the shopping bag swinging at her side. They were almost back at the elevator to the parking lot when Carolina stopped and pressed her nose to the storefront window of a card shop.

It was one of those stores that smelled of pumpkin-spice candles, where glitter coated the floor. And in the window was a set of two teacups, each with a dainty pattern of roses and vines. The handles were embossed with gold, and they were fit for fairies.

Carolina weighed the choices in her mind. Tea set now, or paints someday.

She'd have to convince Mami to order paints, if there was no place to buy them near Larksville.

She'd have to convince Mami that paints were important, even if you were just making do.

She'd have to convince Mami to let her use her birthday money.

"I want that tea set," Carolina said, going into the store.

"A tea set? What for?" Tía Cuca followed her in, laughing as the door made a jingling sound to let the shopkeeper know they were there.

"It's just a game Jennifer and I are playing," Carolina said, hating the way *playing* sounded, like *Run along and play* or *It's only a game.* Then, feeling she needed to add an explanation, she said, "The game's about—"

"Tea with the Queen!" Tía Cuca finished for her. "I love that you still keep your imaginative games, Caro."

"Really?" Carolina had been expecting the almost-in-middle-school lecture.

"Yes," Tía Cuca declared lavishly. "Hang on to that as long as you can, Caro."

Carolina handed the cashier the bills. While he counted out the change, Gabriela watched her with a knitted brow.

But Carolina ignored her. She had a tea set for the cabin and Tía Cuca's seal of approval. Someday, Caro thought, she would make up for the sheets.

At camp, Carolina and Jennifer found more ways to sneak away to the cabin, and each time, the cabin became more of a home, bright and cozy. One day in late July, Yuan and Josh took both groups to visit the cows in the far pasture, and Jennifer and Carolina peeled off to the woods before anyone noticed them. They finished painting that day, and the cabin was transformed into a trim and tidy cottage. The following Tuesday afternoon, while Jennifer's mom worked late, they hiked to the cottage and Jennifer built miniature houses for the elves out of sticks and rubber cement. Now the hearth was not just a village but a universe; Jennifer laid streams of blue pebbles and oceans of green moss. That weekend, Carolina made colors, not with oil paints but with everything she had, everything she found: the red ballpoint pen, dollar-store watercolors, a couple of broken crayons and half-dry poster paints from Jennifer's collection.

"If you'd just ask my dad—" Jennifer protested.

But Carolina's flamboyán bloomed without him, and page after page of trees and oceans and Ratoncito Pérezes and goldfish and saints burst into color.

Every night, Carolina showed her drawings to Gabriela, who learned important things—where Abuela Carmen, whom Gabriela barely remembered, had stored the chocolate Kisses, and how the yagrumo leaves were green on one side and silver on the other.

Carolina stayed up in the kitchen with Gabriela when the grown-ups went outside or upstairs. She showed her cousin how to make a ketchup-and-mayonnaise dipping sauce, whose absence in upstate New York baffled Carolina, and which Gabriela proclaimed delicious. They stirred chocolate powder into their milk, and Carolina was shocked at how perfectly it dissolved: at home, there had been clumps that withstood even the most vigorous stirring. "It must have been the humidity that made it so hard to dissolve," Carolina said, surprised.

"See?" Gabriela said. "That's another thing I don't know about, what humidity does to chocolate powder. When we go to Puerto Rico, I'm going to drink nothing but chocolate milk." And so they added it to the growing list of things Gabriela would see and do the next time, on their someday trip to San Juan.

Carolina didn't tell Jennifer about her midnight meetings with Gabriela, or the shy new friendship between the two of them. It wasn't that she thought Jennifer would mind, exactly. It was more that now her life had two parallel tracks, each its own separate road: Jennifer and the cottage in the forest, Gabriela and the late-night conversations in Tía Cuca's kitchen. Carolina liked it that way, her two little worlds.

By the last week of July, it was scorching hot even in the early morning, before camp started. On the playground, Carolina gathered her hair in one hand and fanned the back of her neck.

"You need to braid it, like mine." Jennifer searched her pockets and pulled out a hair elastic. "Gosh, your hair is thick, Caro."

Carolina had thought that Uncle Porter was wrong, that she would never be glad of the air-conditioning, but today she could barely wait to get into the artificially cold camp center. Hot in New York was different from hot in Puerto Rico—it suffocated.

When free time came, no one wanted to go out. Yuan

came over to their table with a box full of art supplies. "Jenn will be happy," she said, unloading felt and clay and glue onto the table. "We're going to have extended art time today."

"Yeah, but how am I supposed to make anything with this place so packed?"

Carolina stared at Jennifer. It was unlike her to resist art supplies for more than thirty seconds, and even more unlike her to whine.

Jennifer leaned over and whispered, "Don't blow my cover. I'm giving everyone a rational explanation for why we don't want to craft."

Alyssa raised an eyebrow at Jennifer. "So now you need a private studio?"

Gabriela busied herself with the art supplies, keeping her eyes focused on the ball of clay she was kneading and not responding to Alyssa.

"That's right, I do." Jennifer got up and dragged Carolina toward the kitchen area in the back of the camp center. On the counter Lydia had propped up a binder with *Rogan Realtors* on the spine, and she was engrossed in reading. Before Jennifer could say anything, George came out of the back room and dropped a manila folder in front of Lydia.

"Finally got those conservation people off our necks," George said. "They should stop calling you now."

"Thanks, George," Lydia said softly, then sighed.

Carolina looked between Lydia and George, wondering who could possibly be calling to bother Lydia. Everyone in

Larksville loved her. Before she could ask, Lydia turned to her and Jennifer.

"What can I help you girls with?"

Jennifer leaned over the counter and flashed all three braces colors at Lydia.

"Can Caro and I go explore the farm, Lydia?"

Yuan's head turned sharply their way, and Carolina suddenly remembered how Yuan had looked at them the day they'd decided to stay out in the rain. Luckily, the little kid Yuan was helping got sick of wiggling a fork in the glue, unscrewed the cap, and started pouring the glue onto his project.

"Devin, no! It'll get everywhere!"

Lydia glanced at Jennifer, then at Carolina. "As long as you're together, I don't see why that should be a problem. Stay in the shade, it's a hot day." She went back to her paperwork.

They ran down the path, ignoring the heat and Jennifer's cheeks, which got redder and redder as they went.

They came to an empty pasture and Jennifer ducked under the fence. "It's quicker if we cut across here." She tugged on Carolina's pant leg and told her to follow, but Carolina had frozen in place.

"It's George," she hissed at Jennifer. "He must have left the camp center right behind us, and he *definitely* sees us!"

"Where?" Jennifer straightened up and shaded her eyes.

George lumbered down the path, leaving deep boot prints in the dirt. He was whistling. "Wandering again, girls?"

Jennifer suddenly started twirling in place, lifting her face to the sun. "It's just so peaceful in this pasture," she said. "Carolina and I decided to come here and dance."

George shook his head. "Suit yourselves. I'm headed to my car. Don't let me hear that you were out of bounds, though."

When his back was turned, Jennifer stuck her tongue out. "*Nothing* is out of bounds at Silver Meadows, that's what Lydia used to say. We're *neighbors.*"

"He's awful," Carolina agreed. "I don't understand how someone as nice as Lydia could be someone like George's mom."

George glanced over his shoulder, and Jennifer resumed her dramatic twirling.

"We'll have to wait here a few minutes, at least until he's out of sight," Carolina said nervously. "I hate lying to Lydia."

"We're not lying," Jennifer said confidently. "We're just going a *little* bit off the trail. Besides, the way to the cottage is like our own trail. Just because it's not marked doesn't mean it's not a real path."

George was not in a rush, and twice he looked back at them. Carolina joined in on Jennifer's dancing each time, and she saw George shaking his head in the distance, no doubt grumbling about people who twirled in fields on scorching-hot days.

When George had been gone a long time, they cautiously made their way to Cooke's Hill. The heat made everything drowsy and still, even in the forest. It seemed to Carolina that all the living things, the birds, the squirrels, even the deer, were too warm to move or rustle and chirp like they normally did. Even as the girls approached the cottage, there was no sound of the tarp flapping in the window, and no jingle of the wind chimes, only mosquitoes buzzing around them. For the first time since she'd found the cottage, Carolina felt like she was trespassing in the woods. It was so silent that it was like nearing hallowed ground, whose sanctity they ruined just by being there.

Jennifer gripped Carolina's elbow with her free hand.

"Caro." She pointed.

The leaves cast a dancing pattern on the cottage, and in between the shadows, the fresh paint gleamed, clean and white. The pond was still.

But the door to the cottage was open, just a crack. A sliver of blue light escaped from inside.

"Maybe it was an animal," Carolina whispered.

Jenn put her finger to her lips. "Animals can't turn knobs," she breathed, and Caro remembered how Jenn carefully closed the door whenever they left the cottage, pulling the knob tight. Caro remembered the *click* of the latch catching each time they said good-bye.

The door was still, the tarp's blue light steady on this breezeless day.

Finally, Caro whispered, "I'm going in."

Jennifer squeezed her elbow tighter. "You can't," she hissed back. "What if it's a robber?"

Carolina loosened her arm from Jennifer's hold. "There's nothing in there to rob," she hissed. Holding her breath, she tiptoed across the tiles.

There was a squeaking sound as Carolina pushed open the door all the way and crossed the threshold of the cottage. She put both hands on the doorknob, willing the door to silence itself.

A dark silhouette blocked the blue light of the tarp over the window. The silhouette was tall, and black hair cascaded down its back. It was humming to itself, a tune Carolina recognized, but this figure had changed it, made the same tune slower: *Cha-cha conmigo,* it sang sadly.

Carolina's jaw dropped. "Gabriela?"

"Hi, Caro," said Gabriela.

"What—what are you doing here?"

"Just don't be mad."

Carolina swallowed. She wanted to be mad, she wanted to yell at Gabriela for trespassing into her private world, her perfect, secret world.

"What are you doing here?" she repeated.

Gabriela shrugged. "I just wanted to see what you were up to."

Jennifer burst through the door. "Carolina! Are you okay—?" She stopped in her tracks when she saw Gabriela.

"It's fine, Jenn. It's my cousin."

"What are you doing here?" Jennifer asked suspiciously.

"Nothing," Gabriela said. "I didn't touch any of your stuff, I promise. I haven't even sat in your chairs. I was bored, okay? Alyssa isn't talking to me because I told her to keep her big mouth shut about how I look, and I can't talk to Jamie when Alyssa's around because you know Jamie just does whatever Alyssa wants, and I *knew* you had been sneaking off somewhere all summer."

"What did you do, track our footprints?" Carolina asked.

"Of course not. It wasn't that hard. Yesterday when I saw you leave I followed you. I wasn't being secret, honest—I just saw you crossing the stream and knew you'd probably gone into the woods, and you know everyone's worried about us being here since Paul died, and then when I saw you leave the trail I got *really* nervous, but then I saw you come in here and it looked—I don't know—safe."

"How did you get here so fast?" Carolina asked. "You were still in the camp center when we left!"

"I took a shortcut," Gabriela said. "I could tell George was going to catch up with you, so I skipped the cow land and cut through the fields."

"*George,*" Carolina groaned. "He held us up."

Jennifer was still hanging on to the door. She hadn't yet set foot in the cottage. "You never talk to me," she said to Gabriela suddenly. "We've been going to the same camp since we were really little and you never talk to me. Now you want to follow me to *my* cottage? Look, I'm sorry that Little Miss Angel Pants isn't talking to you—"

"Jenn, knock it off!" Carolina held up her hands in a truce. "Gabriela's my cousin, remember?"

Gabriela flipped her hair over her shoulder. "It's not your clubhouse, anyway, Jennifer."

"It's not a clubhouse at all!" Jennifer shot back. "It's an artists' house! You can't just come here to gossip and read magazines, you know."

"Who said I was going to read magazines? I've sworn them off, anyway." Gabriela crossed her arms. "I'm saying it's not your clubhouse—okay, *artists'* house, whatever you want to call it—because the farm belongs to Lydia."

"How do you know we aren't on my parents' side of the hill right now?"

Gabriela shrugged. "Just a guess."

Nervously, Carolina inched over to the left, putting herself in between Jennifer and Gabriela, who were glaring at each other. Jennifer looked like she was about to cry. "Does it really matter? Lydia wouldn't care if we were up here."

Gabriela knelt in front of the fireplace and examined the elf figurines.

"Don't touch those," Jennifer said.

"I wasn't going to touch them. They're cute." Gabriela sat back on her heels. "Look, even if Lydia doesn't care that you're here, she'd want you to *share* the clubhouse, wouldn't she? It's not fair if you don't let anyone else up here."

"Well . . ." Carolina looked at Jennifer. "She has a point, Jenn."

Jennifer stomped outside. Carolina and Gabriela followed her, and found her sitting on the burnt-orange tiles, staring at the green pond. "You're just ganging up on me because you're cousins."

Before Carolina could answer, Gabriela strummed the wind chimes, and a cascade of music sounded, like a waterfall, or a stream running by.

"Caro. It's like your house—wind chimes." And Gabriela looked around, at the tiles and the green pond and up at the sky that could not be seen through the canopy of trees, and said, "Just like the terraza. All you're missing are the goldfish."

Gabriela understood the importance of this place to Caro—in her little cottage, in the depths of these woods, Caro felt close to Puerto Rico, and to home.

Gabriela gave her a pleading look. "Alyssa will get over it soon. I just want to hang out a little while. Just until then."

Carolina rubbed her temples and sat down next to Jennifer. "What do you say, Jenn?"

Jennifer shook her head. "It's like Alyssa Rogan owns the whole world."

Gabriela swung her tote bag over her shoulder. "She doesn't own me. Look, Jennifer, I won't bother you. I could talk the counselors into giving us free time tomorrow. Everyone trusts me—*I* haven't been sneaking out in the rain and the heat and every other chance I get. I bet I could even get Lydia to give us packed lunches to bring up here. We could spend practically the whole day tomorrow."

Carolina remembered Yuan, and the sharp jerk of her head when she and Jenn had asked permission earlier that day. She thought of Tía Cuca's house, of the hectic talking and the sterile cleanliness, and the yard, flat and exposed. All Carolina wanted was for this woodsy cottage to stay hidden, to remain her secret spot. Maybe Gabriela was right; maybe they needed her cover.

"Pretty please?" Gabriela pressed Jennifer. "I could help with your fairy village. My mom has these little houses—"

"Elf village," Jennifer corrected her.

Gabriela cracked a smile. "So I can come back tomorrow?"

"Not a peep to anyone, though. You can't tell your friends."

Gabriela zipped her lips and threw away the key, but she looked over Jennifer's head at Carolina, and she couldn't stop the grin from bursting out anyway.

Chapter Thirteen

Tía Cuca drove them home from camp that afternoon, and when they got to the house, Mami thrust open the door. "Guess what?"

Daniel launched himself toward Mami and she scooped him up.

"What?"

"I found a job!"

Gabriela immediately put down her backpack and kissed Mami's cheek, but Carolina stayed planted where she was.

"Congratulations, Tía Ana," Gabriela said.

"Caro, come here and give me a hug!"

"I thought—I thought Papi was the one looking for a job."

"He is, but this way we'll have a little bit of income, and it's so nice, we'll get to know more people around here."

"What kind of job?"

"It's at the school. One of the teachers had to leave summer school unexpectedly, so I'm taking over her English language arts class, but it may be extended into the fall, if someone takes a leave!"

Carolina tried to sound excited. "That's great, Mami." She fluttered a kiss somewhere near her mother's cheek, then drifted up the stairs, backpack still on.

They were staying. Papi had said there was no path, and yet Caro could see that they'd come to a fork in the road, and chosen New York. Of course, it was what Mami and Papi had said would happen all along, but somehow she'd never really expected it to happen, never expected that they would stay.

Daniel bounced into her room. "Mami got a job!"

"Daniel, don't you realize what this means?"

"What?"

"We're not going back. We're not going home to Puerto Rico."

"Yeah, because we moved here."

"But don't you miss home?"

Daniel wiggled onto Carolina's bed, then lay down, his chin propped in his hands. "I don't know. We'll go visit. But I like it here. There's a whole farm here, and I'm allowed to walk to the pizza store by myself here, and we have a yard—"

"It's not our yard, we're just sharing it until we get our own place."

"Yeah, but all the houses here have big yards, even the

little ones. Ben has, like, six big trees." Daniel spread his arms like tree branches. "Really wide ones. Oak trees—those are the ones with acorns."

There were acorns on Cooke's Hill. Even at the height of summer, acorns and brown leaves decorated the forest floor. Come fall, the hill would burst with color—and at the thought, an image of the cottage wrapped in autumn yellow and fiery crimsons sprang into Carolina's mind, and against her will she felt a leap of excitement. For the first time in her life she would see the autumn of cartoons and of picture books, the autumn of changing leaves and crisp air. She brushed the thought aside, guilty at her own disloyalty. "But, Dani!" she protested. "At home we had a terraza, and you had goldfish to feed."

Daniel shrugged. "We could get some goldfish in our new house."

"They'd freeze in the winter!" Why didn't Daniel understand? After all she'd done, getting the ratoncito and everything, he didn't even seem sad.

A dreamy look passed over Daniel's face, and Carolina knew she wouldn't be able to reason with him, wouldn't be able to bring him back down to earth.

"Ben and I are looking for elves in our yards. They can talk to squirrels, you know."

"What about the Ratoncito Pérez? He's Puerto Rican. There's no Ratoncito Pérez in New York."

Daniel gave Carolina a puzzled look. "Um, yeah there is. He gave me ten whole dollars, remember?"

At dinner, everyone was talking at once. Uncle Porter toasted to Mami, and Daniel clinked his spoon against his glass until Gabriela told him to knock it off. But she said it in a way that made Daniel laugh, and Carolina wished she were like that, wished she were more buddy-buddy when she told Daniel to stop.

Tía Cuca called for music, and the next thing Caro knew, Chiquifancy's music blasted from the speakers and her family was a blur, everyone dancing the Fancy: Mami with Papi, Uncle Porter with Gabriela, Tía Cuca with Daniel.

"Come on, Caro!" Tía Cuca stepped to the left, clapped, and sang to the music, *"Cha-cha conmigo,"* motioning for Caro to join her.

Carolina sat up straight. The kitchen reminded her of family parties in San Juan. There weren't quite as many people, not the crowds that used to appear at Abuela Carmen's on holidays, but they were celebrating just as merrily. Mami pulled Caro to her feet, and Carolina wished she wouldn't. Now they were all sliding to the right and shimmying, and Caro felt ridiculous. She wanted to sit and listen again, to let the music carry her away into memory.

Then the song shifted, and where Chiqui's bright rhythms had been, there was now Cuban music: the flute, sweet and high. Mami and Papi swayed together, and they were like a breeze on the terraza, damp from the sea. Carolina could almost feel it on her skin.

"Let's go see a movie this weekend to celebrate," Tía Cuca said when the song ended.

Everyone launched into what was playing and what they wanted to see, but Carolina noticed Papi's silence when he and Mami parted. He sat in a kitchen chair, staring into space while the others looked up movie times on their phones and loudly recounted previews. Carolina scooted closer to him. "You're next," she said quietly, so no one else could hear. "You're going to find something soon." She kissed him on the cheek.

His smile was a little sad, but it was real. "I'll figure something out." He placed his hand over Carolina's, his ring shining under the high spotlights of Tía Cuca's kitchen. "Acuérdate—"

"Caminante, no hay camino."

Carolina thought back to those blurry days of packing, when there had been no time for drawing, no time for dreaming, only days of helping Mami, rushing to get things into suitcases or to relatives or into storage. She wondered what would happen to that storage unit. She'd labeled the cardboard boxes so carefully, writing out their contents in her neatest handwriting on each side.

Papi had played his music, setting his phone down on whatever surface he could find, and taking it with him when he moved to another room. It had annoyed Mami, the way she kept finding the music in unexpected places. But it was something Carolina loved about Papi. She hadn't heard that music for weeks now, and with a sharp inhale she realized that she wanted her family to find their own place, a place where Papi could leave his music on in every room. Carolina realized that Papi, too, had been playing perfect in Tía Cuca's house.

Papi smelled like hair gel and violets, and he pushed away the scentless sterility of the house, pulling Caro close to him. Carolina hummed, then, in the absence of the music that had been there a moment ago, she sang softly, sang the Caminante song.

"What are you singing?" Gabriela asked curiously.

Before Papi could answer, Carolina explained. "It's a song my dad likes. It comes from a poem by Antonio Machado." And Carolina set about teaching Gabriela.

> Caminante, no hay camino,
> > *Traveler, there is no path,*
> se hace camino al andar. . . .
> > *you make your path by walking. . . .*
> Caminante, no hay camino,
> > *Traveler, there is no path,*
> sino estelas en la mar.
> > *only your wake upon the sea.*

Fairly pleased with her translation, Carolina let Gabriela think about the words. Then, with a flip of her hair, Gabriela announced, "I want to learn it in Spanish."

"Are you two talking about poetry?" Mami called from the sink, where she was loading the dishwasher. "I tell you,

Gonzalo and Caro," she said to Tía Cuca, "you'd think they were the English teachers, not me."

Tía Cuca cleared Papi's and Carolina's plates and brought them over to Mami. "We're lucky to have such smart kids, Ana."

"Caro is bright, isn't she?" Mami said.

Carolina stopped to watch them for a while. She saw Mami smile as she ran the plates under the water, and she knew that as casual as Mami kept her tone, she was bragging about Carolina and Papi. Mami was proud, and Carolina basked in it before turning back to Gabriela and repeating again, *"Ca-mi-nan-te."*

So they were staying, Carolina thought as Papi told her more about Machado, the Spanish poet who himself had moved somewhere new, written his poems about a land that wasn't his own. They were staying, and somehow, Carolina would find her path.

That night, there was a storm, a huge downpour of rain so loud it could be heard in the house, and thunderclaps whose *booms* shook Carolina's chest. Daniel ran into Caro's room at the first sign of the storm, and they stayed awake for a long time, huddling close when the lightning illuminated the windows with its electric blue.

The next day was perfect, which made Gabriela's job at camp all the easier. As soon as lunch was over, she sauntered up to Lydia. "Do we have a lot of activities lined up, Lydia?

Because this is the sort of day you just want to soak in, isn't it?" She motioned to the windows, where the sky was clear cerulean.

Lydia glanced at her clipboard. "Your group was supposed to have barn cleaning, and the little kids were going to do some gardening—but I do have Brian all day today—"

Alyssa inadvertently helped them out. "Have Brian do it, then! It's his *job*. The rest of us are supposed to be having fun, aren't we?"

Lydia wrinkled her nose and looked like she wanted to argue with Alyssa, but then she shook her head. "You kids are just angling for more free time, aren't you? Well, all right." She clapped her hands, and everyone turned toward her. "By special request," she announced to the camp, "I'm giving you the whole afternoon off from activities. It's a gorgeous day and you can all go enjoy yourselves around the farm. But"—she whistled for attention—"if I hear anything from the counselors about you giving them trouble, then we go right back to our scheduled activities, okay?"

Everyone cheered, and Lydia ushered them toward the door. "See you all at three o'clock for dismissal!"

The sky was so clear that Carolina wished she could stop and paint it, an enormous canvas of blue, all blue. She didn't want to look down, even as she followed Jennifer past the tetherball and swing sets to the far gate, sensing Gabriela close behind them.

Suddenly, Jamie sidled up next to Gabriela. "What do you want to do now, Gabs?"

Carolina looked over her shoulder, prodding Jennifer to stop.

Shockingly, Alyssa was nowhere to be seen, and it was just Jamie, in a plain T-shirt, blue like the sky, smiling innocently at them.

"I'm not hanging out with you and Alyssa today," Gabriela said stiffly.

Jamie's face clouded. "Are you still mad at Alyssa? She told me you were mad. It's not her, though, Gabs, it's her parents—"

Before Jamie could finish her sentence, Alyssa came hurrying toward them. "Jams! What are you doing?"

She stopped short when she saw Gabriela.

"Hi," Alyssa said tersely.

"Hi," Gabriela replied.

Alyssa adjusted her barrette, pink as always. Her hair was fine and straight, not a strand ever fell out of place, and Carolina wasn't quite sure what the barrette was supposed to be doing. For the first time, she wondered if maybe the barrette was someone else's choice. Carolina hadn't met Alyssa's mom, but she was getting the impression that she was a pink-barrette kind of person.

"What are you going to do today?" Alyssa asked.

"Oh, you know, just hang out with my cousin." Gabriela threw an arm around Carolina.

Alyssa nodded, too quickly. "Did you talk to your dad about the Chiquifancy concert? Is he going to take you?"

"I have no idea what you're talking about." Then, with a

flourish, Gabriela added, "It's not like my family really *likes* Chiquifancy or anything. Why would you think that?"

Alyssa's eyes grew wide. "I just thought—maybe your dad would convince my dad. You know, we had said . . ." Alyssa thrust something into Gabriela's hand. "I made this for you."

Gabriela was flabbergasted.

Since Alyssa usually spent craft time talking, Carolina couldn't help her curiosity. She leaned over to see.

It was a necklace, with a pendant made of cardboard and glitter. Chiquifancy's face was pasted on, then heavily layered with clear gloss. It looked pretty good—trendy, and something Gabriela might actually wear.

"Since we've been having all the extra craft time. I thought you might like it, but if you're not into Chiqui anymore—"

Gabriela suddenly found her voice. "I'll put it on right now." She tied it around her neck and fingered the diamond-shaped pendant. "Thank you. If you wanted, you could—"

"Come over after camp!" Carolina finished for her, taking Gabriela by the shoulders.

"Really?" Alyssa stepped toward them.

"Yeah," Gabriela said, "or you could come—"

"Help Brian!" Carolina said, in a stroke of brilliance.

Jennifer chimed in, "You know, it's a hot day, and it's really not fair to Brian. *Someone's* got to scrape the poop in the barn, and it might as well be us."

Alyssa stopped in her tracks, Jamie alongside her. "Oh," she said. "Well, I'll call you after camp, Gabs."

"Yeah," Gabriela said, still holding the pendant.

They made their way vaguely in the direction of the barn at first, looking over their shoulders constantly.

"Is Alyssa going to follow us?" Jennifer asked nervously.

Gabriela shook her head slowly. "No. She doesn't like barns. Alyssa's more like a city person even though she's from Larksville."

As they made their way down the path and Gabriela expertly swung herself over the fence and followed Jennifer through the tall grass, Carolina realized that Gabriela, in her own way, was a country girl too.

They crossed the creek and hiked to the cottage. Gabriela hummed Chiquifancy songs to herself, and Jennifer and Caro were silent.

"You know, you don't have to stay with us," Jennifer said as they reached the burnt-orange tiles. "You've already gotten us the extra time."

"I want to. It's just—" Gabriela stepped over the threshold of the cottage. "Maybe we could invite Alyssa and Jamie to come next time?"

"What?"

Carolina dropped her backpack in one of the chairs. "It's supposed to be a secret. We agreed yesterday. You promised!"

"Yesterday I didn't know Alyssa *wanted* to hang out."

"But—Jennifer and I come here to work."

"You're eleven. You don't work."

"Just because you're thirteen," Jennifer said defensively, "doesn't mean you can tell us what to do."

"I'm not telling you what to do," Gabriela burst out. "I just want to invite my friends, and you aren't letting me!" She turned to Carolina, her hair whipping around as she did. "When you moved here I had to invite you everywhere. My parents wouldn't let me do anything without asking you to come. And now— Oh, forget about it." Gabriela stormed toward the door. "I'm going to go get Alyssa. See you in a while."

"Gabriela!" Carolina screamed, but Gabriela had taken off into the woods.

They ran after her, but Gabriela had a lead on them. Her long legs carried her farther and faster, and she was out of sight in a flash. They sprinted in the direction she'd gone, but it was impossible to keep it up, and they fell into a panting and exhausted heap.

They were totally off the trail now, and beneath the trees, this crystal-clear day was actually a little chilly. The dry breeze on her sweaty skin surprised Carolina.

"Hey!" Carolina stooped and picked up a dirty white ribbon off the ground, still breathing heavily. "Isn't this one of our trail markers?"

Jennifer took it and held it up. "It is," she said slowly. "But we're not anywhere near there; we've been walking across the hill, not down it."

Carolina scanned the trees around them, trying to orient herself. "The storm must have carried it away last night." Tentatively, she called, "Gabriela?"

There was no answer.

"Here." Jennifer took the ribbon and tied it to the nearest pine tree. "At least we know this spot."

They wandered on, looking for anything they recognized, calling for Gabriela. Caro remembered the first time she'd been in the woods alone with Jennifer, how Jennifer had told her to walk more quietly. Carolina hadn't understood at first, but now she hated to be shouting, to be so loud amidst the trees. It violated something; she thought it was like skipping stones on a pristine lake. It ruptured.

After a while, they stopped and sat down on a tree stump. The moss was wet, and she knew it would leave a brown, damp mark on her jeans, but Carolina was so tired she barely cared. "What time is it, Jenn?"

Jennifer checked her wristwatch. "Three-forty-five."

"What!" Carolina leapt to her feet. "Camp ended forty-five minutes ago! We missed dismissal?"

Jennifer nodded, and Carolina noticed that there was nothing stuck in her braid that day, that it was all Jennifer's hair.

"I guess we should just start walking downhill. We'll find the farm eventually, right?" Caro asked nervously.

But the hill leveled flat after only a few feet. They kept walking a long time, but before they caught any sight of the creek or the farm they found themselves at the top of a small ledge, and below them was a clearing, with a pond at its center, framed by cattails almost as tall as they were.

"Do you know where we are?"

Jennifer shook her head. "Silver Meadows is a big place," she said softly.

A cow mooed in the distance, and Carolina followed the sound with her gaze, past the pond and back into the trees. "Let's go that way."

"But we have to get back to the camp center."

"What time is it?"

Jennifer checked her watch. "Four-fifteen."

Carolina's heart sank. "Come on." Carolina took off toward the sound of the cows. "We have no way of knowing which way is the camp center, but we can find the cows, and they have to come get the cows soon. Otherwise we could be stuck here forever."

Jennifer swallowed hard, then steeled herself. "Okay. Lead the way."

The reeds were so tall that they could see only a few feet in front of them. They heard Gabriela before they saw her, crying softly beside the pond.

"Gabriela?" Carolina knelt beside her. "Are you lost too?"

Gabriela wiped her nose with the back of her hand. "Yes. And now we're all in huge trouble." Wet with tears, Gabriela's eyelashes were incredibly long and black. Carolina wondered if she would ever look like Gabriela, if being cousins meant that in two years she, too, would be tall, with long hair and eyelashes that went on and on.

"I can't believe you got us into this mess." Jennifer's arms were crossed, and she hovered over them without sitting.

Gabriela wailed, "I just wanted to show Alyssa the clubhouse—"

"Artists' house," Carolina corrected her automatically.

"I thought she'd think it was cool!" Gabriela sobbed, burying her head in her knees.

"Why do you have to do everything Alyssa's way all the time?" Jennifer fumed.

"She's her friend, Jenn." Carolina looked up at Jennifer, who was scowling. "You'd want to show me too. Wouldn't you?"

Jennifer's face softened slightly, and she loosed her arms, letting them swing at her sides. "Still . . ."

"Look," Carolina said, "we're all in this together now. If we don't make it to the cow field, we're going to be camping here tonight." She reached under Gabriela's arm and lifted. "Come on. Up."

There was a tender spot in Caro's heart now, when she thought about the cottage, about the questions she knew were coming. But it was late. The air was cool and the light was soft, dismissal had come and gone. If they could only get back to the farm . . .

They were slow and quiet, listening for the sound of the cows and adjusting their course each time they heard another moo or the jingle of a bell. They reached the far end of the clearing and entered the woods once more. Gabriela was still sniffling as she walked.

"Ga-aabs! Jenn-ifer!"

"They're calling us!" Carolina said excitedly. "Over here!" she shouted. "Come on!"

"That was Alyssa's voice," Gabriela said uncertainly.

"Jenn!"

A grin broke over Jennifer's face. "But *that* was my dad! They must have sent out a whole search party!" She waved her hands wildly, and through the trees there appeared Alyssa, Gavin, and Lydia. George was behind them.

Chapter Fourteen

Everyone in the camp center was talking at once. Alyssa was with her dad, Lance, who, for someone who controlled so much, was smaller than Carolina had expected. Lance was barely taller than Alyssa, with thinning brown hair and thick glasses. Alyssa was carrying on about how worried she'd been while George loudly complained that kids today had no discipline. Gavin rested a hand on Jenn's shoulder while Lydia boiled water for tea and scolded herself about giving the kids so much free time. In the corner, Mami and Tía Cuca looked small, clutching their purses and sitting at the far table. For once, they were silent.

The kettle whistled, and Lydia poured mug after mug of tea. She carried them over to the table, then she pulled out some chairs. "Sit," she told everyone.

Carolina sat down across from Mami, avoiding her eyes. Lydia settled at the head of the table.

"So," Lydia said. "Do you want to explain yourselves?"

Caro racked her brain for an explanation. "We got lost," she said finally.

"Carolina, maybe you got lost, but these two"—Lydia pointed at Gabriela and Jennifer—"know better than to leave the trail. After what happened to Paul! We were out of our minds with worry!"

Alyssa clasped her hand to her heart. "I was worried *sick* about you, Gabs."

"You were?"

"Jenn, we've told you to stay on the trail a million times," Gavin said. "I don't understand why you would go off like that."

Jennifer stared at her hands.

"If none of you will give me a reason . . . ," Lydia warned.

"It was my fault," Gabriela said. "Jenn and Caro were following me. It wasn't their idea."

"Then do you want to tell us *why* you led two younger girls so far off the trail?" Lydia asked.

"And your father and I will have something to say to you when we get home, young lady," Tía Cuca added.

Gabriela hung her head. There was an awkward pause, then Lydia sighed.

"Given what you did, Gabriela—"

"Wait." Jennifer got to her feet. "It wasn't Gabriela's idea." Her cheeks were bright red. "She's just sticking up for us."

"See, Daddy?" Alyssa whispered. "I told you it wasn't Gabriela."

Lydia turned to Jennifer. She was very quiet. "I must say

I'm surprised. I thought *you* out of everybody would understand why we have these rules. Do you want to give me an explanation, Jenn?"

Caro's heart was breaking for Jennifer, who was sitting there just like Gabriela: head down, hot cheeks, looking ashamed. Caro took a deep breath.

"Jenn and I like to go to the woods during free time," Caro said. She searched for a plausible reason for getting lost, something that wouldn't make Gabriela look bad. All eyes were on her. George, Alyssa, Lance—they wanted an explanation. She thought of the search party in the woods, combing the land, looking for them. Sooner or later, they would discover the cottage.

It might as well be from her.

"It was because—"

She stopped. Jennifer and Gabriela both looked up, and they subtly shook their heads. Carolina wished she could think of some other reason to give, but her mind was drawing a blank. She opened her mouth again, but before she could go on, George dropped a blue folder on the table.

"Ma, enough. We don't have to listen to this. By next week, all these problems will be long behind us—and good riddance, I say."

Lance Rogan chimed in, "I think your son is right, Lydia. Our offer couldn't have come at a better time."

Gabriela looked between Lance and George. She wrinkled her forehead. Then she jumped to her feet. "You're selling the farm!"

"Gabriela!" Tía Cuca said, shocked.

"You are!" Gabriela stomped over to Lydia. "How could you? You can't sell Silver Meadows! I've been coming here every summer since I was six! My cousin Caro just *got* here!"

"And you're my neighbor!" Jennifer piped in. "I don't want to live next to more—" She looked daggers at Alyssa's dad, then crossed her arms and settled back into her seat.

"Girls, calm down," Lydia said.

But as she spoke, Carolina felt her pulse quickening. She longed for her sketchbook, still lying in her backpack on the floor of the cottage, longed for the peace of the woods and not the chill of this too-full room, where everyone was angry, and where Mami just stared at her without uttering a word.

"George and I decided to sell the farm several weeks ago," Lydia explained. "Lance has made us a very generous offer, and you know I can't keep up the farm forever. That's why he was here today after camp, before your absence at dismissal interrupted us."

"I'm sorry," Mami said, finally talking. "Caro's usually such a good girl. She's usually so helpful."

Carolina bit her lip, wondering what had happened to her, how she had gone astray. Mami was right. When else had she lied to a grown-up, wandered off the path, snuck tooth money past her own parents, and stolen bedsheets from her aunt?

Lydia patted Mami's hand warmly. "I'm not mad, Ana. Kids wander off sometimes. I'm just sorry this decision took everyone by surprise."

Mami squeezed Lydia's arm. "I understand your difficulties. Sometimes it's right to let go. I felt that way when we came here."

But what about the cottage? Carolina thought. She couldn't stand imagining it empty or, worse, torn down like their house in Puerto Rico. She wondered what Alyssa's dad would do with Silver Meadows, whether it, too, would become straight streets and new houses.

Lydia put down her tea and came around the table. She put an arm around Carolina. "Honey, don't cry. It was time for me, and for Silver Meadows. Things aren't like they used to be. Without my husband, I'm alone."

"You have neighbors," Gavin said.

Lydia smiled. "Wonderful neighbors, but it's not the same. Farms take a lot of work. I can either keep Silver Meadows as a shell of what it once was, or I can let it go. Those are the choices. Two roads have diverged in my little wood. Do you all know that poem?"

Softly, Lydia recited:

> *Two roads diverged in a yellow wood,*
> *And sorry I could not travel both*
> *And be one traveler, long I stood*
> *And looked down one as far as I could*
> *To where it bent in the undergrowth.*

"That's Robert Frost again," she finished. "His farm wasn't so far from here, you know."

Politely, Carolina nodded, but inside her mind she responded, simply, *Caminante, no hay camino.* She didn't want to look at Lydia, because she knew she wouldn't be able to stop the tears then. So she just blinked, and wiped her eyes, and nodded again.

Lydia rose, patted her on the back, and settled into her seat. "Okay, girls, new rules for the last week of camp. One: You stay within sight of the camp center at all times."

"What?" Jenn complained.

"Two: If you want to go past the playground, you bring a counselor. I don't want you to think I don't want you to explore the farm; that's the whole reason I have this camp. But from now on everyone would be more comfortable if you stuck with a counselor."

"Don't worry, Lydia, I'll keep an eye on them," Alyssa said.

Mami interrupted them. "No, that won't work."

"Tía Ana," Gabriela said.

"No," Mami said again. "Lydia, you've been very sweet, but I don't want Caro going off anywhere, with or without a counselor. It's not like her to get in trouble, and if this is what happens when she gets a little bit of freedom, from now on I'd prefer if Caro stayed at the playground or the camp center. That is my wish."

"Mami—"

"Caro, you want independence, you have to earn it."

Carolina thought again of her sketchbook. The secret of the cottage was safe a little while longer. But if she could never return there with Jennifer, never draw or dream there again, she might as well have told the truth.

Tía Cuca and Mami had a lot to say in the car as they rolled onto the main road, right past the turns that led to dirt roads and farms and woodlands, until they reached Tía Cuca's house.

"Gabs, you really embarrassed me this time." Tía Cuca turned off the engine and unbuckled her seat belt. "If it wasn't bad enough that you made us worry so much, to talk to Lance Rogan like that!" She held open the door to the back seat.

"I know how to open a car door, Mom."

Tía Cuca jerked her head toward the house. "Inside. We are not done discussing this."

Gabriela didn't move. "What is there to discuss? You heard Lydia—we're not allowed out of her sight for the next week. There's nothing else to talk about."

"I'll see you inside, Gabriela."

Gabriela jumped out of the car and followed Tía Cuca halfway across the lawn. "I can't believe you're doing this to me!" she shouted. "Alyssa's just starting to be friends again and now I'm going to be on a leash—like some kind of criminal!"

Tía Cuca stopped just before the entrance to the house, her face white. "I seem to recall Alyssa saying she'd help keep you in bounds, Gabriela. And given how you've been acting, I'd say that's a good thing."

Their voices faded away as they neared the front door and then entered the house. Carolina and Mami were still in the car, and just as Carolina was unbuckling her seat belt, Mami told her to close the car door.

Carolina leaned over and pulled it shut. Gabriela had left it hanging open, so most of the cold air had escaped, and with the sun beating down on the roof, the temperature inside climbed quickly. A single mosquito had gotten in, and it buzzed close to Carolina's ear.

"You see what you did?" Mami's voice was very quiet, and her face was set straight ahead. From the back seat, Carolina could see the little hairs that grew at the back of Mami's neck, and how her neck arched to her ears, which were different from Carolina's: they were flush with her head, dainty and small. Carolina had Papi's ears, the kind that stuck straight out, as if God had almost forgotten about them and then hastily smacked them on.

"Tía Cuca was humiliated in front of her husband's boss, Caro. And your cousin, who's done nothing but try and help you fit in, is in trouble now."

"Gabriela was out of bounds, too, Mami!"

"So now you're saying it's her fault?"

Carolina shut her mouth tightly. Better to say nothing and not anger Mami more. She wanted to say that they wouldn't have gotten into this mess if Gabriela hadn't goaded Jennifer—but everything Carolina could say would only set Mami off further, only convince her more that Carolina had done this all on purpose.

Mami took her purse, which had been balanced neatly on her knees, and put it on the dashboard. Deliberately, she turned to face the back. "If this is your behavior when you're with Jennifer, then I don't think she's a suitable friend for you, Carolina. I can't have you going to play with someone who might lead you into the woods—or worse. Cuca told me what happened to Lydia's husband. Did you know he went off the trail and—"

"I know!" Carolina blinked back tears for the second time that day. "I know that. But Jenn is nice, Mami. The first week of camp she was the only person who really talked to me. And, Mami, she's an *artist*—like me."

"Ay, Caro. Por favor. Being an artist doesn't matter now."

"How could you say that? You used to take me to Señora Rivón's—you *liked* that I was an artist."

"Of course I *like* it, it's that—" Mami shook her head. "What I meant is that it doesn't matter—*nothing* matters—if you're not safe. You should have good friends. People who don't get you into trouble."

"I got myself into trouble," Caro said softly. She watched the mosquito, buzzing around the headrest, until her eyes crossed. Mami still spoke, but in Carolina's mind the only sound was this mosquito and her own voice: *I'm an artist, I'm an artist. It always matters, being an artist.*

Mami was leaning farther into the back seat, until Carolina's eyes refocused and settled on Mami.

"Caro, we're just starting to make things work here. Papi has a second-round interview next week. Do you understand what that means?"

Carolina nodded.

"I'm not letting you ruin everything with one bad friend-ship. This is a small town. Everybody talks."

Except it didn't seem small to Carolina; it seemed vast and open, the rolling hills were like the ocean. She'd never known there was so much space anywhere but the sky.

She nodded again, then slowly stepped out of the car. Jennifer, her first real friend, the artist, the daughter of a real painter—it had all come together so quickly, and now it was so quickly over. She couldn't believe it. Mami had turned up her nose plenty of times, asked questions and dropped comments, but she'd never actually forbidden anything before. Then again, Carolina couldn't think of another time when she'd done anything but try to be perfect and keep every rule that Mami made.

She pulled open the front door of the house. This was one of the things she liked about upstate New York, the way no one locked their doors. Of course, the door kept the house practically hermetically sealed, but at least if you pulled hard enough, it opened. At home, the house had breathed, let in air and sound. But it could also feel like a series of cages: the locked front door behind the locked gate, the high iron rails all around the house, and the gate that led out to the main street. Each one required its separate key. Carolina had been like that before, studious and rule abiding, letting in Mami, Papi, Daniel, door by door. That house had allowed in so many sounds and smells but no one like Jennifer, no best friends, no artists to share the bench beneath the flamboyán.

Daniel was watching TV in the living room, something

Mami normally didn't let him do on weeknights, even in the summer.

"Caro! I was worried about you!" He ran up to her and wrapped her in a hug. Carolina held him tightly.

"Did you really get lost in a forest? Were there bears? Tell me everything!"

Daniel had already had his bath; his hair was slicked to one side, and Carolina drank in the clean, violetas smell of his head. "No bears," she said. "There was nothing to worry about. Just an accident."

"Oh no! What kind of accident?"

"Everyone's fine now," Caro said, hugging him.

She wandered upstairs after that, and knocked on the door to Gabriela's room. She could hardly remember whether she was mad at Gabriela, whether they were on separate teams these days, or the same.

"Come in."

Gabriela was at her usual station, cross-legged on the floor with her laptop balanced on her knees. But the room was different now: the magazines had been cleared away and the path across the floor was empty.

"Hey!" Gabriela was surprisingly chipper.

"Thanks for sticking up for us," Carolina said. "You didn't have to take the blame like that."

Gabriela shrugged. "Sorry I got you lost in the first place. I shouldn't have—I just missed Alyssa so much."

Carolina sat down on the floor across from Gabriela. "Did you get in big trouble?"

"Not that bad. My mom just had to get it out of her system. Besides, Alyssa's mom called practically as soon as we got inside and they invited me to go to the lake with them next weekend, so my mom knows her dad's not mad." Gabriela rummaged through the tote bag on the floor next to her and pulled out a lollipop. "Candy?" she asked cheerfully.

Carolina took the lollipop and set it on her knee. "What's going to happen to Silver Meadows?"

Gabriela hesitated. "Lydia has to sell the farm sometime, doesn't she? And people like the neighborhoods Alyssa's dad builds," she went on. "They need places to live."

But there wouldn't be forests, Carolina knew, or cottages hidden by trees, or the sounds of wind chimes and cowbells guiding them through the trails and paths of the farm.

She sighed. "So you and Alyssa are friends again now?"

"She was worried about me. Isn't that sweet?"

Carolina didn't understand it, but then she didn't understand Alyssa—didn't understand her interest in Chiquifancy concerts or her dislike of spiders or her artificially high-pitched tone. Still, Carolina didn't know what it was to have a friend since forever, someone whose friendship stretched over years—she thought that, when Gabriela looked back, she wouldn't see a wake on the sea or a path in the woods but something sharp and sturdy: a paved road, and Alyssa laying the cement.

"But what about those things her parents said?" Carolina asked.

"Well," Gabriela said thoughtfully, "she can't help what

her parents say. But she doesn't have to think the same things. She made me that necklace, and she told me she's going to tell her dad that he was wrong about Chiqui—and me."

"That's brave of her," Carolina replied, and she meant it. She didn't know what it was to tell your dad he was wrong, to stick up for her friend.

If she were Alyssa, she would probably wear barrettes forever.

"What Alyssa's parents think of me is their business," Gabriela said wisely, then immediately spoiled the effect by sucking loudly on her lollipop. "They don't have to like the same music as me for Alyssa and me to be friends."

Carolina looked down at her own lollipop, at how hard and dry it looked compared to Gabriela's slick one. "I'm not allowed to see Jennifer anymore. My mom just said so."

Gabriela swallowed hard and pulled the lollipop out of her mouth. She placed it on the floor, without even setting it back in its wrapper. Carolina cringed at the mess, but with a confident toss of her hair, Gabriela said, "Caro, I think Jennifer is the weirdest kid I've ever met. But if you want to be friends with her, then be her friend. You can't always do whatever Tía Ana wants you to. Sooner or later, you're going to have to stick up for yourself."

Part Three

Caminante, son tus huellas
    el camino, y nada más;
Caminante, no hay camino,
    se hace camino al andar.
Al andar se hace camino,
    y al volver la vista atrás
    se ve la senda que nunca
    se ha de volver a pisar.

Caminante, no hay camino,
    sino estelas en la mar.

Traveler, this path is a wave upon the sea,
    only your own wake, and nothing more;
Traveler, there is no path,
    you make your path by walking.
By walking you make your path
    and when looking back,
    you see the road
    you'll never pass again.

Traveler, there is no path,
    only your wake upon the sea.

                —Antonio Machado (1875–1939),
                    "Proverbios y cantares XXIX"

Chapter Fifteen

The days dragged on and on. July turned into August, and at camp, Carolina kept her head down, borrowing paper from the art supply closet and spending free time drawing inside. She'd dreaded having to tell Jennifer what Mami had said, but without their trips to the woods, she found that she and Jennifer didn't have much time to talk. It wasn't even that Lydia's new rules kept them from going back to the cottage, it was that Lydia herself was transformed. The day after they got lost, she had tacked the easel paper that listed the day's activities onto the wall, and she now followed it meticulously, checking her watch constantly to make sure they transitioned at exactly the listed times. She posted a new schedule every day, and every day their afternoon free time was shorter and shorter, until camp felt like a factory assembly line. They moved from crafts to garden to swimming like clockwork, but there was no joy in any of it.

One day Lydia gave them fifteen minutes before dismissal, and Carolina settled at her now-usual station, drawing at the table indoors. Jennifer sat down next to her and pulled out the felt figure she was making, while Yuan stood nearby, between their table and the window. Carolina watched as Jennifer worked. She squinted and hunched over when she was focused, and Carolina noticed that these days she was weaving colorful strings of beads into her braid. It reminded her of sea princesses, with starfish and pearls in their hair, but when she opened her mouth to say so, Jennifer motioned to Yuan. Of course she thought Carolina wanted to talk about the cottage, but there was nothing they could say, not now that the counselors wouldn't let them out of their sight.

At Tía Cuca and Uncle Porter's house, it was as if everything had gone back to normal, to before the mishap in the woods, but Carolina sensed the differences that no one mentioned out loud. Mami had thrown herself into teaching wholeheartedly, spreading her students' assignments out on Tía Cuca and Uncle Porter's dining room table every afternoon, and once she went out to dinner with the other teachers. She came home that evening flushed and happy, eager to repeat their stories to Tía Cuca, who just as eagerly took in any tidbits of town news that Mami could share with her. There was a flurry of activity surrounding Papi's interview, too: Uncle Porter asked Papi practice questions, and one rainy day Mami picked his suit up from the cleaner, making sure to keep it under her umbrella.

Gabriela was back to spending all day at camp with Alyssa

and Jamie and messaging them every second they weren't to-gether. Gabriela wore Alyssa's Chiquifancy pendant every day, but Carolina noticed that her magazines never reappeared.

Best of all, when Jamie's birthday came around, the sparkly dress emerged.

"Are you sure you don't want to come to the party?" Gabriela asked as she changed her dangly earrings.

"Nah, I want to read tonight."

"Suit yourself."

Gabriela had stopped trying so hard to pull Carolina into her circle, and she was nicer for it. After Jamie's party, she sat with Carolina on the deck, cheering Daniel on as he leapt around the yard trapping fireflies in a jar.

A few days before camp ended, the campers moved their chairs away from the tables, making a circle that stretched all the way around the camp center, while Lydia perched on a stool. Carolina thought how she had never met anyone quite like Lydia, someone who could be so dignified while wearing work boots, whose hair was gray but whose voice was bright and whose body was strong. She envied Jennifer a little bit, for being from a place like Silver Meadows, a place where people were painters and farmers, where people's history stretched back for generations. *Stay on the trail,* Lydia had said, because Silver Meadows was all well-worn paths.

"As you all know," Lydia began, "last spring my husband, Paul, passed away."

There was a stir among the campers, and Daniel crawled into Carolina's lap, where she held him as Lydia told her story.

"Paul loved Silver Meadows, and so I've tried to keep the farm alive, especially having all you kids. Camp was the highlight of Paul's year, his whole life long.

"But I've come to a fork in the road."

Carolina watched the faces of the kids around her. She watched them wiggle in their chairs and twirl their hair. Some of them had been coming to Silver Meadows every summer for years. She wondered if they knew what Lydia was about to say, and she wondered what they would do next summer.

"As some of you have already heard, I have a chance to sell Silver Meadows. It's a chance to start a new life, one that I hope will bring me joy—" Lydia rubbed her eye. "Some of the joy that's been lacking." Lydia's face was suddenly blank, and Carolina was struck by her eyes, how wide they were, big and round.

"There was a bit of poetry my husband and I used to like. Paul loved Robert Frost, a poet who was also a farmer, and we learned this one as children. We always thought of it when it came to decisions."

Carolina steeled herself, and Lydia began once more,

"Two roads diverged in a yellow wood . . ."

And in Carolina's mind again the response arose, *Caminante, no hay camino . . .*

"And sorry I could not travel both,"

You make the road by traveling.

"And be one traveler, long I stood,"

A traveler is a walker, a caminante.

"And looked down one as far as I could

To where it bent in the undergrowth."

But Carolina didn't see the road like Lydia did; she didn't see it going on and on. Now Carolina saw like Papi saw it: white crest of salty water, foam and mist, a wave upon the sea, and one foot in front of the other. Cuba, Puerto Rico, New York, Carolina's roots were not in the soil but in the rhythm of her family's movement, step after step.

"I've come to a place where the roads diverge, and decided to sell the farm—"

Kids cried in outrage, and Carolina joined them, though of course she had already heard what Lydia was telling them. She wished that Lydia could see anything but this crossroads, one choice or the other, with no possibilities beyond.

That night Carolina couldn't sleep. Robert Frost and Antonio Machado went round and round, their words chasing each other: *Two roads diverged*—no—*Caminante, no hay camino*, the poems argued in her head, looping through her mind again and again, interspersed with worry about Papi's big interview. The interview was tomorrow, and Carolina knew that Papi wanted this job from the way he cleared his throat whenever it came up: it was almost like a nervous cough, which Papi tried to stifle. Papi was ready, but something was missing. It gnawed at Carolina, made her jittery and kept her wide-awake.

She finally kicked off the covers and went downstairs.

Papi was already down there, reading silently by the light of a single lamp.

"Papi, don't you have to go to bed? You don't want to be tired tomorrow."

Papi pulled a bookmark off of the end table and carefully marked his place. He put the book down without making a sound. "I should, but I couldn't sleep. Neither can you, it seems."

"At home we would have prayed before your interview," Carolina said. "And we would have lit a candle next to the virgencita so that she could help you tomorrow."

Papi smiled and rose to his feet. "Tía Cuca must have a virgencita here somewhere." He took Carolina's hand, and she felt small and safe as he led her through the dark rooms of the hollow house. "Tía Cuca and Uncle Porter are Catholic, too, you know."

"But they don't have any statues or saints," Carolina said. At home, the virgencita had been there always, standing over the goldfish, and inside Mami had kept the Caridad del Cobre, the virgencita who had appeared to fishermen in Cuba, on her dresser to watch over their family. The saints had been mixed up in every part of their lives, but here the church seemed far away, something you did on Sundays and forgot the rest of the week.

They came to the kitchen, and Papi led her into the garage. They found one box labeled *Christmas,* and another labeled *Nativity,* like Tía Cuca's neatly marked sewing bins.

"There has to be a María in here," Papi said. "She'll be happy to come out a few months early."

She was porcelain, and a little cheesy-looking, but Carolina hoped the real virgencita wouldn't mind. They carried her into the kitchen and lit a single birthday candle at her feet, and Carolina prayed in front of the counter, closing her eyes tightly.

Meanwhile, Papi took out his phone and played his music. The whistle of the Cuban flute wove its way into her, behind her eyelids and into her prayers. *Let Papi get the job. Let him get it.* The music and the prayers brought the lapping of the water in the little fountain to her mind, and made the gulf between here and there feel small and insignificant.

Papi put his hand on her shoulder. *Let him get it, let him get it.*

She realized now that she wasn't praying for only Papi; she was praying for herself, for the growing part of her that wanted to be here, in Larksville.

They blew out the candle, which made the kitchen smell of ice cream cake. And after that, they both slept soundly.

The evening before their last camp day, Carolina and Gabriela sat at the kitchen island eating pistachios and spitting the shells into a bowl. From time to time Gabriela's phone would light up with a new message from Alyssa or Jamie, which she would respond to with one hand, but most of the time the screen was dark. Everyone was waiting for Papi to hear back from his interview, which meant Mami and Tía Cuca were cleaning everything in sight, anxiously scrubbing and polishing each already-pristine surface of the house.

Tía Cuca was putting away the dishes and Mami was wiping the counter when a door slammed out front. Tía Cuca looked up from the dishwasher. "Are you expecting a friend, Gabs?"

Gabriela shook her head just as the doorbell rang.

They all went to the front window, as if the news about Papi's position would be coming by mail, and looked at the pickup truck that had just pulled up in front of the house.

"I have a toy truck just like that," Daniel said conversationally. "Except mine's red, and we didn't bring it to New York." He tugged on Mami's sleeve. "Did you put my red truck in storage, Mami?"

Mami shook her head, still staring out the window. Jennifer was walking through the hedges, down the path toward the front door of the house, while her dad waited in the car.

"I'll go talk to her dad." Mami handed the dishtowel she was holding to Carolina.

Before Mami could get to the entry, Daniel bounded to the door and opened it a crack.

"Who's there?"

"Daniel!" Carolina pulled him away. "You're supposed to ask that before you open." Uncle Porter and Tía Cuca might leave their doors unlocked, but she thought Daniel should probably still get in the habit of asking.

Mami came up behind them, and Carolina let herself

fade into the corner, holding Daniel by the shoulders. She heard the engine of the truck start again, and through the paneled windows on either side of the entry, she saw it rumble away, leaving Jennifer alone.

Jennifer stood in the doorway, not asking to come in, just standing there.

"Jennifer," Mami said stiffly. "How nice to see you."

"Hi. Can I see Carolina?"

Carolina gripped Daniel's shoulders more tightly. A part of her wanted to shout hello, but another part of her wanted to shrink even farther into the corner, and disappear.

Mami sighed. "Jennifer, Carolina can't come play right now."

"I know you're mad at me for getting Carolina in trouble," Jennifer said, "but I promise that won't happen again. I've never, *ever* gotten into trouble at camp before, and I've been going there since I was eight years old. Can't I talk to Carolina for five minutes? Just five minutes? *Please?*"

Carolina saw that Mami was considering, torn between not wanting to say no to Jennifer's face and not wanting to give in. "I think that's enough for now, Jennifer," said Mami quietly.

"Mami, wait." Carolina let go of Daniel, and he ran away, back to the kitchen. "I want to talk to Jennifer. I think I should be allowed to."

Mami raised her eyebrows. "You haven't exactly inspired trust and confidence, Caro."

"But we'll stay right here this time. We're not going to

go anywhere, we're just going to hang out at the house. Tía Cuca said I could have a friend over, remember?"

Shyly, Tía Cuca came into the entry. "I did say that, and I meant it."

Mami paused, and Carolina tried to make her face look angelic, as angelic as Alyssa looked with her pink barrette. Mami checked her watch. "Okay, girls. You can talk for a little while, then Carolina has to help us get ready for dinner and I'll drive Jennifer home. Agreed?"

"Deal!" Carolina thrust the door open the rest of the way, resisting the urge to give Jennifer an enormous bear hug. She grabbed Jennifer by the wrist. "Come on, we can go to my room." For the first time, she was grateful for the bare, sterile room in the big house, now that she had Jennifer to share it with.

In Carolina's room, with the door shut firmly behind them, Carolina did squeal with happiness. "I've missed you!" she gushed, surprised at the sound of her own voice. She sounded like Tía Cuca.

"Me too." Jennifer took off her backpack and dropped it on the floor. "Lydia has us on such a tight leash, we can't talk about anything anymore." She turned to Caro. "I just wanted to see you again."

Carolina breathed in deep. Shyly, as if she and Jennifer hadn't been friends all summer, she said, "My mom is taking us to register for school next week. Maybe we'll be in the same class."

"Classes," Jennifer corrected her. "Middle school, re-member? We start changing classes every period next year."

A rush of joy flooded Carolina, one like she hadn't felt in months, maybe ever, at the thought of going to school, and of having a best friend. Gabriela was right: Mami could think what she wanted, could like different houses and different clothing, but that didn't change Carolina and Jennifer. Carolina knew right then that she would always find a way to be with her best friend.

Sunlight bounced off her desk, and Carolina noticed how the wood gleamed without the familiar presence of her sketchbook to soften it. Melancholy crept back, and she looked at the floor. "What about the cottage? What will happen to it?"

Jennifer laughed darkly. "I don't think Rogan Realty is going to keep it."

There was a sharp rap at the door, and Gabriela let herself in the room, shutting the door behind her. "I couldn't help overhearing what you were saying."

"How?" Carolina asked. "That door is, like, made of titanium!"

"I was listening in," said Gabriela without a trace of guilt.

"Gabriela!" Jennifer said.

"I have an idea."

"Gabriela," Jennifer protested, "If you hadn't gotten us lost—"

"Please, you were just as lost as I was." Gabriela hopped onto Carolina's bed. "I had an idea about how to save Silver Meadows. It just came to me last night."

"Does it involve your and Alyssa's dads not buying the farm?"

"Jennifer, that wouldn't work anyway. Come on, you have to admit that Lydia *wants* to sell the farm. She's old. She's tired. She's sick of cleaning up after cows."

"You make it sound so awful," Jennifer muttered.

"But here's the thing," Gabriela said. "Someone *else* might want to farm that land one day."

"They can't, not if there are a bunch of new houses," Carolina said.

Gabriela grinned mischievously. "That's just the thing. What if Lydia made sure that it *can't* be filled up with houses, even after she sells it?"

Something clicked in Carolina's mind. "You mean"— *what were they called*—"the conservation people?"

"Exactly."

Carolina turned to Jennifer. "Do you remember that day we were asking Lydia permission—George said something about the conservation people?"

"My dad talks about them all the time," Gabriela went on. "They buy the rights to farm on the land, so even if Lydia moves, or sells it, the land has to be used for woods and farms. Sometimes all of it, sometimes just a part." Gabriela beamed. "Isn't that a great idea?"

Carolina wrinkled her brow. "But if the conservation people already called Lydia, why didn't she just *do* it?"

The house phone rang, and Carolina jumped to her feet. It could be Papi calling from his cell phone. He might have heard about the job already. She opened the door and ran to the top of the stairs, Jennifer and Gabriela close behind her. Listening intently, all they could hear was Mami saying, "Uh-huh" and "Okay" from time to time. Her voice didn't reveal any emotion.

When Mami had been silent for a few moments, Carolina called out tentatively, "Mami? Ma?"

Mami appeared at the bottom of the landing and rested one foot on the second step. She shook her head. "No news yet, Caro."

"What are you waiting—"

"Oh nothing, Jennifer," Mami said in a pathetic imitation of a light and airy voice.

"I'll tell you later," Carolina mumbled to Jennifer. "Okay, thanks for letting me know, Mami."

Back in her bedroom, Carolina filled in Jennifer while Gabriela went to get her laptop.

"My dad's been applying for jobs, and he had an interview that he's supposed to hear back from soon. I don't think my mom likes talking about it outside of the family—she thinks it's embarrassing or something." Carolina shrugged. "But I don't mind you knowing. You're my best friend."

"I've never had a best friend."

"Me neither," said Carolina. Then she added quickly, "If you don't want—"

"No. It's awesome." All three rubber-band colors and every square of metal in Jennifer's mouth shone.

Gabriela came back with her laptop and started looking things up furiously, hitting the keys with gusto.

"Umm, Gabs?" Carolina asked.

"Hmmm?"

"Your idea is great and all, but have you thought about why Lydia wouldn't have already done that? There must be a reason."

"See!" Gabriela ignored Carolina's question and motioned for them all to gather around her. "There are lots of websites about how to protect the land for farming."

Carolina looked over Gabriela's head at Jennifer, who said, "Send me that page, Gabriela. I'll look at it when I get home."

Gabriela slammed her laptop shut. "When you get *home*? We don't have that kind of time. You need to do something now. Lydia wants to sell the farm right after camp ends; I asked my dad."

"But that doesn't give us any time—"

"Which is why I'm telling you now. I can't do anything," Gabriela went on. "My dad works for Rogan Realty— but you two can do whatever you want. You can convince Lydia."

"But how?" Carolina asked.

Gabriela tucked her laptop under her arm. "I don't know, but you didn't get the idea from me, remember? Ta-ta!" She waved, and shut the door behind her with a thud.

Chapter Sixteen

Carolina and Jennifer kept talking and debating what they could do to influence Lydia while the evening sunlight turned to blazing orange. It was almost dinnertime when Papi knocked on the door. His face was unreadable.

"Did you hear?" Carolina asked eagerly.

"Well, all your prayers must have helped, because I got the job!" He spread his arms wide, and Carolina leapt to him.

"Congratulations!" Jennifer shrieked, thumping Carolina on the back, as if it had been Carolina's own achievement and not Papi's.

Gabriela appeared in the doorway and hugged Papi congratulations too. "My mom wants you to come down for a drink before dinner," she told him, and let herself back into Carolina's room.

"This means you're a real Larksviller now!" Jennifer said to Carolina. "Are you excited?"

"I guess so. I mean, I'm really happy for my dad." Carolina bit her nail. "I just wish I had my sketchbook." It was hard to process anything without it; everything was rushing by.

Gabriela looked toward the desk, as if Carolina might have just overlooked the sketchbook, hiding in plain sight.

"It's in the cottage," Carolina explained. "I left it there that day when we got lost, and now I can't go back for it."

"But you need that sketchbook," Gabriela said. "It has all of those drawings of Puerto Rico, you can't just leave it. What if an animal gets in there? Or it rains?"

"Well, it's in a backpack," Carolina said defensively.

"Is that why you haven't had a backpack all week?" Jennifer asked. "I thought it was because you were trying to be like Gabriela and Alyssa."

Gabriela snorted. "By not carrying a backpack? Is that what you think we're like?"

Jennifer pointed to Gabriela's tote bag, which was slung over her shoulder. "You and Alyssa and Jamie always wear tote bags, not backpacks. I figured it was because you thought backpacks were uncool."

"Yeah, because they make you hunch over."

"See? I told you."

"Whatever you say, Jenn. See you later." Laughing to herself and shaking her head, Gabriela closed the door.

"I actually agree with her," Jennifer said. "You were going

to make a painting from that sketch of the tree, remember? For decoration."

"But now . . ."

"We'll have to find a way to get that sketchbook back," Jennifer said simply.

Mami was so overjoyed by Papi's news that she forgot altogether about taking Jennifer home, and Jennifer stayed for dinner. She and Daniel had a long conversation about the differences between elves and fairies, Daniel's eyes growing wider with every word Jennifer spoke. Across the table, Carolina noticed Mami listening in.

"Elves have curly toes," Jennifer said seriously.

Mami's brow wrinkled with worry. Then Jennifer wiggled Daniel's sandal. "They're curly like this!" she joked.

Daniel burst into peals of laughter, and Mami half smiled. She leaned back in her chair and watched them a little longer before turning to Papi. "Felicidades," Mami said to him. "Felicidades."

Contentment washed over Carolina.

The last day of camp was hot but dry. When Carolina's group went out to feed the pigs, they kicked up puffs of dirt as they worked, and Carolina felt tiny prickles all over her skin in the barn, where dust seemed to be rising off of the hay bales. After lunch, the counselors took them on one final tour of the farm, to say good-bye to all their favorite spots. Some of the animals had already been sold, and Carolina marveled that she hadn't noticed before how the herd had thinned out these last two weeks.

Lydia made a speech back at the camp center, wishing them well, and then it was all over. The campers hugged and said their good-byes, some of them making plans to meet by the lockers when school started, or visit the lake one last time before summer's end.

Carolina dragged her feet on her way to the car, where Tía Cuca and Mami were waiting. She lifted her eyes slightly, just enough to see Gabriela and Dani climb in the car, then lowered them again and drooped her shoulders. With her right hand, she gave Jennifer the signal.

"Caro! Caro!" Jennifer came running up. Her face was red, and she held her side in a remarkably good imitation of being out of breath. "I was just in the camp center and Lydia is *crying*. She's so sad about camp ending!"

"What's this?" Tía Cuca rolled down the window and leaned over Mami. "Something's wrong with Lydia?"

"She's really upset," Jennifer said.

Tía Cuca reached for a package in the back seat, in between Daniel and Gabriela. "I'm so sorry to hear that. I have a little gift for her, but we were going to wait until next week to give it to her."

Mami propped her chin up on the dashboard. "It's lovely here at Silver Meadows," she said. "It's so peaceful."

Carolina and Jennifer looked nervously at each other.

After all summer, *now* Mami decided to notice how beautiful Silver Meadows was?

"It is peaceful," Caro said. "That's why Lydia's so upset." Suddenly their story sounded silly, and Caro tried to telepathically communicate to Jennifer that they should abandon the plan, but Jennifer plowed full steam ahead.

"I was going to pick Lydia some wildflowers," Jennifer said. "Do you think she'd like that?"

"Oh, that's a wonderful idea!" Tía Cuca gushed.

Mami nodded her head slowly. "You know, Jennifer, you're very thoughtful."

Caro squeezed Jenn's hand. She could hardly believe that Mami was buying it.

"It was so hard to sell the house in Puerto Rico," Mami went on, "and we hadn't lived there our whole lives. It must be terrible for Lydia."

"That's why we want to help," Jennifer said. "Maybe—maybe Carolina could help me with the flowers?"

Mami pursed her lips. "I just don't want you girls wandering off again."

Gabriela leaned forward from the back seat. "There are a lot of flowers right on the path by the camp center, Tía Ana. Lydia loves those flowers too. I think it's a great idea."

Mami leaned back and considered Gabriela. Carolina held her breath. Mami wasn't like Tía Cuca; you couldn't just pull anything over on her—

"Should we wait here?" Mami asked.

Tía Cuca suddenly punched the dashboard to see the

light-up clock. "I have to stop at the pharmacy before they close! We have to go now. Girls, we'll come right back and pick you up." She started the car, then seemed to remember Mami in the passenger seat.

"Is that okay, Ana?"

"I guess so," Mami said. "But, girls, if I hear *anything* about you in the woods—"

"We'll be good!" Jennifer promised, and waved wildly.

They watched the car roll away.

"We did it!" Jennifer gave Carolina a high five.

"But if we get in trouble today—we really can't get lost—my mom will never let me out of the house again."

"We won't, we're just going to get that sketchbook and come right back."

"Let's move fast."

"Don't worry," Jennifer said. "I know the pharmacist. They'll be in line forever."

All the same, they ran down the path, grateful for the dry day; it was impossible to move quickly when it was muddy. They crossed the stream in a rush, their feet pounding against the wooden planks of the bridge, making a racket as they raced up the trail, stepping on twigs and crunching leaves left and right. As they veered off the trail and turned toward the cottage, Carolina could almost feel the weight of her sketchbook filling her hands. Each time her feet hit the dirt, she thought, *I'm coming, I'm coming.*

The cottage came into sight, and Carolina's heart leapt. She wished she could fly the rest of the way. They hurried toward it, and pulled open the door as Jennifer called, "Helllooo, house—"

Jennifer stopped, still hanging on to the doorknob, and Carolina nearly ran into her. It was the second time they had been surprised in the cottage, and this time it wasn't Gabriela's silhouette but a bright yellow cushion that took them aback.

The cushion was fluffed and perched on the right-hand chair, giving the cottage a cozy, overstuffed look. There was a box of crackers in between the two chairs. The flaps of the box were open, and the plastic bag poked out from within.

Carolina remembered all at once the first day she'd seen the cottage, how she'd envisioned the elves playing in the fireplace at night, or dancing to the rhythm of the wind chimes. She remembered the old woman in her rocking chair on the terraza, looking out at the pond, where goldfish maybe swam. The dream was coming true. Carolina saw that woman in the form of the gray-haired person who was sitting and staring into the unlit fireplace.

"Lydia?" Jennifer's voice was barely at a whisper.

Lydia's smile was soft; it welcomed them in. Jennifer sat on the free chair, and Carolina perched on its arm. The metal vines dug into the back of her thigh, but she paid them no mind.

"So it was you two," Lydia said, unsurprised. "The new paint looks wonderful, I must say."

"We were going to do more," Jennifer said. "Hang paintings and stuff. But now—"

"I didn't give you the time," Lydia finished for her.

"Lydia?" Carolina asked timidly. "How did you find out?"

"George was going to tear the cabin down this week. They'd asked us to do it before the sale—it's falling apart, you see." Lydia pointed to the ceiling, where a patch of dry leaves poked through from the roof.

Jennifer grabbed Carolina's hand and squeezed it. Everywhere, everything was being torn down.

"Imagine my surprise when I discovered that old Cooke's cabin, long since empty, had been tidied and furnished, a little jewel of a home."

Carolina hung her head. "We're sorry, Lydia. We just—we got carried away."

Lydia looked around at the cottage. "This cabin's been here since my parents bought the farm. It was Old Man Cooke's, you know. The one for whom the hill is named. I used to come often, but I've been so busy lately—keeping things up by myself, you know. I haven't been by in months, and then I find . . ." She motioned to the curtains, and the scene in the fireplace, then smiled to herself. "I used to play here as a child. For us kids, this was quite the clubhouse."

"Artists' house," Jennifer said automatically.

"Oh yes." Lydia leaned forward and picked out an elf from the figures in the fireplace. "You make such beautiful things, Jenn. And, Carolina, I've noticed you're an artist too."

Carolina gathered herself, summoning her strength, and announced, "Yes—I am an artist."

"She draws," Jennifer explained. "That's why we came here today. Carolina left her sketchbook."

"Understandable."

Carolina picked up her backpack. The thick nylon had kept the inside mostly dry, but a few of the sketchbook pages were warped, where the dampness had gotten in. Carolina marveled at the dampness, how like the Caribbean this cottage could be in its own way: here as there, the damp could work its way into every little space. Before, Carolina had been obedient—starched and ironed and sprinkled with violet water like her old school uniform, but still the humidity had found her, and things changed.

With the sketchbook clasped tightly to her chest, Carolina approached Lydia. "We wanted to ask you something." She laid the book on Lydia's lap. "See, when we moved here, someone bought our house in Puerto Rico, and they tore it down, and it broke my heart. It wasn't just that the house was beautiful—it *was* beautiful—but it was also magical. I had my own drawing spot, my own place under the trees." Carolina flipped to the drawing of the flamboyán. "It was where I listened to the birds and wind chimes, and even the traffic from the road. Now it's not there anymore." Carolina took a deep breath. "My mom and dad had to move, even though they didn't really want to. But I think you have choices, and you should use them."

Carolina had talked so much that the quiet seemed odd in contrast, the way she could hear every breeze that hit the tarp. Someone was walking outside; their heavy steps punched down the soil. Before Lydia could speak, the sound drew closer, and George ducked through the door.

"Ma, what are you doing here? I've got to get all this stuff out for the demolition, remember?"

"Just chatting with some old friends, George."

George scratched his head. "What are you girls doing here?" He shook his head. "If camp weren't over, you'd be in for a talking-to."

"I just wanted to say good-bye to the place one last time," Lydia said.

"But maybe you don't have to say good-bye!" Jennifer protested. "You could keep it! Just don't sign the contract, Lydia."

George threw up his hands in exasperation. "Really, girls, the nerve of you! It's a done deal."

Lydia closed the sketchbook and handed it back to Carolina. "I wish we had a choice, girls. But it's either sell or keep farming, you know that. I'm much too old to keep farming, and George has another life in Albany. There's no one to take over the farm."

"But what about the conservation people? They called you, didn't they?"

"How did you know that?" Lydia asked. Then she shook her head. "Someone could fall—be injured."

"Is that what you've been worried about, Ma?" George drummed his fingers on the windowpane. "I thought you—"

"What?" Lydia asked, turning to face her son.

"I thought you needed more money for it," George

mumbled. "But if it's just that, we could fix that wall, keep people away from the ravine. . . ."

Lydia half smiled. "You don't have time for that, George."

"What if it doesn't have to be one or the other?" Carolina interrupted.

"Carolina—"

"You said that two roads were diverging. But what if there's another road, one you didn't even see? Or no road at all. My dad always says that we make our paths by walking."

Lydia fixed Carolina in her gaze. "I think your dad is very wise, honey, but in this case—"

"What if you could sell the farm but keep some of it as farmland? Isn't that like another road?" Jennifer dug in her pocket. "Here, we printed this out for you. Just read it." She thrust the paper into Lydia's hands.

"When you're in the woods," Carolina said, "there are the trails, with markers that someone put up to guide the way. But there are so many trees and so many ways to get around them—just because you can't see those paths doesn't mean they're not there." She knelt down by Lydia's chair. "There's a poem in Spanish, and maybe you've never heard it. It's about roads, but not about roads diverging. It's about finding them." Carolina began the best translation she could muster, the one that she had taught to Gabriela:

> *Traveler, this path is a wave upon the sea,*
> *only your own wake, and nothing more;*

Traveler, there is no path,
  you make your path by walking.
By walking you make your path
  and when looking back,
  you see the road
  you'll never pass again.

Traveler, there is no path,
  only your wake upon the sea.

Carolina stood, and stepped back.

Lydia had listened attentively, then stared again into the fireplace, as if the little elves could give her an answer, or as if the hearth really danced with flames. While Carolina waited for a response, Jennifer took her by the elbow and led her toward the door of the cottage.

"Think about it" was the last thing they said before leaving George and Lydia, alone in the cabin that had once been Old Man Cooke's.

Chapter Seventeen

The house phone rang in the middle of breakfast Saturday morning. Carolina was eating her cereal while Gabriela helped Daniel pick the best blueberries out of the container. Mami and Papi were deep in conversation with Uncle Porter and Tía Cuca about houses and apartments.

Tía Cuca got up to answer the phone. After a moment, she cupped her hand over the receiver. "Porter, it's for you."

"I'll take it in the other room," Uncle Porter said, folding his napkin.

Gabriela stretched, then came over and rested her chin on Carolina's shoulder. "I'm bored," she said.

"You just woke up."

"Can you go get your sketchbook and draw me something? I need to be distracted from boredom," Gabriela said dramatically.

"I thought you were going to the lake."

"That's not for three hours," Gabriela whined.

Daniel scrambled onto the chair next to Carolina. "Yeah!" he piped up. "Draw us something!"

"Okay," Carolina said, pushing in her chair. "But just so you know, I'm not some kind of artwork vending machine."

"But you are," Gabriela insisted.

Carolina grinned and went to grab the sketchbook from her backpack. On her way back to the kitchen table, she faltered. Mami and Papi had joined the kids' conversation.

"Have you seen Carolina's drawings?" Gabriela said.

"Of course I have," Mami replied, in an almost-offended tone. "I used to take Caro to her lessons."

Carolina hugged the sketchbook tight to her chest, hovering behind Gabriela.

"She's been making all these drawings about Puerto Rico." Gabriela grabbed the last blueberry, tossed it in the air, and caught it in her mouth like a jelly bean. She swallowed. "Yeah, there's a flamboyán tree and a Cucaracha Martina and everything."

"I didn't know that," Mami murmured.

Papi turned to Carolina. "Did you finish the flamboyán? Let's see it, Caro."

With one eye still on Mami, Carolina stepped up and laid the sketchbook flat.

Papi pored over the image. "I remember you sitting on that bench," Papi said. "You've really captured it, Carolinita."

Mami stood behind Papi, examining the drawing over his shoulder. "Señora Rivón would be proud," she determined. "Maybe you could draw something to send to her."

"I'd like that," Carolina said.

Mami rested her cheek on top of Papi's head.

"She used to sit out there all day, my Carolinita," Mami went on. "She was always drawing." Mami reached down and rested a polished finger on the red penned-in blossoms of the flamboyán. "I didn't know you'd been drawing home." Mami reached out her free arm, and Carolina took the one-armed hug as Dani climbed onto Papi's lap. "My Carolinita," Mami said again.

Uncle Porter came back to the kitchen with his hands in his pockets.

"Well," he announced. "That was Lance Rogan. Apparently Lydia has decided to delay the sale of the farm."

Mami's face clouded with concern. "I'm sorry, Porter, I hope—"

He held up his hands. "I think it's for the best. She's still very interested in selling, she just wants to go over the finer points. It turns out she's had another offer from a young farmer, with some backing from a local conservation group. It might end up being a split sale." Uncle Porter smiled. "Between us, I'm glad. We all need farmland."

As Uncle Porter turned toward the living room, Carolina spoke up.

"Uncle Porter, wait," she said. "Do you know who made the offer? What the farmer's name was?"

Uncle Porter frowned. "Let me think a minute. Hmmm."

Carolina crossed her fingers.

"Alice? Alicia? Something like that."

Carolina thought of flowers in black plastic containers, and of people and places that *belonged,* the way Jennifer's elves belonged in the cottage. They clicked.

Across the kitchen table, Gabriela flashed Carolina the tiniest of thumbs-ups.

Mami drove Carolina to register for middle school the following week, and on the way back, she pulled over just past the main intersection in Larksville. She dug her cell phone out of her purse.

"Could you call Jennifer to see if she'll have you over for a little while?"

Carolina was dumbfounded. "Really?" she finally managed to ask.

Mami held the phone out. "Dani's at Ben's house, and Papi and I want to go look at an apartment. It would be a big help."

"An apartment?"

Mami raised an eyebrow. "Did you want to go see Jennifer?"

Carolina grabbed the phone. "Yes!" she said, punching in the number. "It's just—"

"I trust you," Mami said simply.

At Jennifer's house, Fiona was out and Gavin was busy in his studio, so they raced through the woods, laughing for no reason. They hiked to the place where the trail ended, and stopped there for a long while.

"Should we go look?"

Carolina hesitated. "What if . . . ?"

Jennifer nodded. "We don't know what will happen. Even if Alicia and Lizbeth get part of the farm, if Mr. Rogan gets this part—"

"He wouldn't really tear it down?"

"He might."

The girls ran back down the hill without visiting the cottage, and tumbled into the kitchen. They didn't talk about it again that day.

Mami and Papi liked the apartment, on the second floor of a house right in the center of Larksville, next to the sturdy brick post office. As soon as Mami and Papi had signed the lease, Mami set about, once again, preparing for a move. She folded all their clothing into perfect squares and borrowed the key from the landlord to scrub the floors herself, even though he swore they had been professionally cleaned.

Mami agreed that Carolina had to return Jennifer's invitation, so Jennifer came to Tía Cuca and Uncle Porter's later that week, one day when Gabriela had Alyssa and Jamie there too. Suddenly the house didn't feel big at all; it burst with people. Jennifer had brought her craft supplies, and she and Carolina spread out on the grass in the yard while Gabriela and her friends lounged on the deck.

As she glued the skirt onto a miniature fairy, Carolina overheard snippets of the older girls' conversations.

"I'm going to convince my dad," Alyssa was saying. "We're going to that concert."

"But—it's your dad," Jamie protested. "He always says—"

"I don't care." Alyssa's voice changed to a loud and conspiratorial whisper. "If Lydia can stand up to him, then so can I."

Carolina leaned back, letting her body settle into the curve of the tree. She picked out a shining bead for the fairy's crown, and thought that there was, after all, one thing that was just right about Rogan Realty's brand-new houses: the distance between this tree and that deck, between those lounge chairs and this glorious pile of pipe cleaners and wool roving and special beads. They were together, and they were each their own.

Their last night at Tía Cuca and Uncle Porter's, Carolina sat at her desk putting the finishing touches on her first drawing of the bench beneath the flamboyán. It was missing something, so she added another figure, another girl sitting beside her, this one with a long braid. She filled in the bright rubber bands of the girl's braces with different pens: the rubber bands and the blossoms were the only colors the drawing needed.

"Caro," Mami said, poking her head in the door, "we have something for you. It just came."

Papi, Daniel, and Gabriela were close behind, and Daniel dropped a parcel, wrapped unevenly in bright green construction paper, into Caro's lap.

"I wrapped it," Daniel said proudly.

"And Gabriela helped us pick it out," Mami explained. "She said it was something you needed for the school year."

Carolina eyed the parcel in her lap. "But why am I getting anything? I don't understand."

"Mi vida, let's just say it's something you've been waiting for," Papi said. "Maybe you've even earned it. Lydia and that farmer worked out a deal, did you hear?"

"Really?" Carolina grinned. "That's—" she faltered. Did Papi know what she and Jennifer had said to Lydia? After all, Lydia was friends with Uncle Porter and Tía Cuca, she might have told them the story, and they would have told Carolina's parents. Would her parents be mad that she'd gone off into the woods again?

"Aren't you happy?" Papi asked.

"I think it's great news." Carolina looked dubiously at Mami.

Mami didn't say anything, didn't offer approval or disapproval, just the slightest shrug. Maybe she was proud of Caro's meddling, maybe she was furious, but that, Caro decided right then and there, was for Mami and Mami alone to know. She tore the paper off the package with abandon.

"Do you like it?

In Carolina's lap were three small canvases and a box of new paints. "I love it," she said.

"Now you can paint some of the things you've been sketching," Mami said. "I would love to see that flamboyán in full color."

Carolina grinned, and after everyone left the room she sat for a long time, holding each paint bottle up to the light one by one, and arranging and rearranging the colors in their case. They were not little-kid paints but real ones. They smelled of home: of Señora Rivón's studio, and of Jennifer's house.

There was a hint of cool weather in the air the day Jennifer and Carolina opened the back door to Jennifer's house and noticed a single bedraggled ribbon on the ground.

Jennifer stopped on the steps. "What's that?"

"It's one of our Hansel and Gretel markers." Carolina stooped and picked up the wet ribbon. "But what's it doing here?"

Jennifer clapped her hand over her mouth. "Caro, *look*!"

Carolina dropped the ribbon and followed Jennifer, who had taken off toward the driveway.

The driveway was piled with things, and Carolina thought at first that the garage had been emptied, but as she drew closer she saw outlines of objects she recognized.

Metal chairs with crawling vines, painted a new and brilliant white.

Yellow curtains cut from sheets, cozy and cheerful.

And a folded note with tidy handwriting:

Thank you for the loan of these chairs and curtains, which did wonders to brighten my home. Like any good neighbor, I thought I should return these items once they were no longer needed. They are yours, and I hope you will keep them a good, long time.

> *With love,*
> *Silver Meadows Farm*

P.S. You will think that I have kept the little elves, but I'm sorry to say that they disappeared into the forest. I trust they will find their paths.

"I guess that means the cottage is really gone," Carolina said, just as a breeze came and whipped the note out of her fingers. It sailed away, and landed somewhere near the base of Cooke's Hill, lost among the trees.

Jennifer picked up one of the yellow curtains. "These would look nice in your new room," she said to Caro, and pressed the curtains into Carolina's hands.

They never found the little elves from the cottage hearth. Every time Carolina saw a flash of hunter green beneath an acorn cap, she thought that she had found one, but on closer inspection, it was always only a deeply colored leaf, and a well-positioned acorn cap.

A note on the poets . . .

In seventh grade, I memorized Robert Frost's poem "The Road Not Taken" as an assignment for my favorite English class. I loved the rhythm of the words, and the image of the yellow wood enchanted me. At home, my family shared other works with me—poems by Latin American writers, and poems that Latin Americans have adopted over the years. Poetry weaves its way into how we see the world, and whenever I was confronted with a dilemma, my family offered, in response to Frost's metaphor of two roads diverging, Machado's metaphor, which tells us that there *is* no road, and that we make our paths with our feet. Machado's wisdom suggests that life isn't programmed in advance, that change, movement, and endless possible directions are the norm.

Machado and Frost were contemporaries, and though they never met in real life, I have always linked them. When they are carried jointly, their words remind me that as I navigate decisions, I can draw on the insights of two languages and two cultures. This is a book about a yellow wood, and it is about the bravery of imagining many possible paths—and about reading Robert Frost and Antonio Machado together.

Luis de León was a sixteenth-century Spanish poet, friar, and professor at the University of Salamanca, Spain. In 1572, he was arrested by the Spanish Inquisition because his translations of biblical texts differed significantly from the norms of his time. University lore has it that when he was released in 1576 and returned to teaching, he began his first lecture with the words "As we were saying yesterday," suggesting that his years in prison were no more than a brief interruption. I like to think that the poetry he wrote helped him maintain his tranquility. His poetry was not published until decades after his death, but today it is widely available in Spanish. I translated the first stanza of his best-known poem, "Vida retirada" ("Peaceful Life"), but if you are interested in reading more of his poetry in English, look for Elias L. Rivers's *Fray Luis de León: The Original Poems* (Grant & Cutler, 1983).

Robert Frost was an American poet who lived from the late nineteenth to the mid-twentieth century. He was born in California but lived most of his adult life in New England. He also spent periods of time in Florida, in Michigan, and even in England, but it's his poetry about rural New England that he is best known for today. I am particularly fond of Susan Jeffers's illustrations of Robert Frost's "Stopping by Woods on a Snowy Evening" (Dutton, 2001) and the collection *Versed in Country Things,* edited by Edward Connery Lathem, with photographs by B. A. King (Bulfinch Press, 1996).

Antonio Machado was a late-nineteenth- and early-twentieth-century Spanish poet. He was born in the city of Seville, in southern Spain, and lived for many years in Castile, in central Spain. The Spanish Civil War broke out toward the end of Machado's life, and he was evacuated first to the eastern coast of Spain and later to France. Like Frost's, Machado's poetry is most associated not with his birthplace but with the place where he spent much of his adulthood—Castile. Machado's poem about a wake upon the sea, "Caminante, no hay camino" ("Traveler, There Is No Path"), is widely known throughout the Spanish-speaking world, and has been set to music. The song Carolina's father would have played is "Cantares" by Joan Manuel Serrat. I translated the first stanza of Machado's poem, and my favorite book showcasing Machado and many other Spanish poets in English is *An Anthology of Spanish Poetry from Garcilaso to García Lorca,* edited by Ángel Flores (Anchor, 1961).

Acknowledgments

When I was growing up, summers were about cousins, and while the specifics of Carolina's life are emphatically fictional, the summers I have spent with my family in New York and in Puerto Rico shaped Carolina's observations of the world around her. I shared with my Schwiep and González cousins Cuban parents, aunts, and uncles who were loud, fiercely tight-knit, and unrepentantly chismosos, while my Otheguy cousins and I shared summer camps, boat trips, countless hours playing in my grandmother's yard, and sporadic drawing or sewing lessons from older relatives.

Our trips to my grandmother's house in Puerto Rico awakened memories within my parents, and it was there amidst the coquís and the metal rocking chairs of her terraza that they told my siblings and me stories about their childhoods in Cuba, and about what it meant to leave. It was there that I felt closest to the Caribbean, this longed-for place at the heart of my family life. I am grateful to my aunts, uncles, and cousins for sharing this world with me, for teaching me everything from the names of the plants in El Yunque to where my grandmother kept her stash of chocolate Kisses. Children of exiles may be always searching for the lost place, but through my cousins I've at least known my parents' sun and salt water, and above all, I've known family ties that transcend distance, culture, and language. In particular, I'd like to acknowledge Amaya Labrador for her careful reading of this manuscript. Amaya is one of those rare first-call kind of people, someone who can resolve whatever you throw her way, and I am beyond lucky to be her cousin.

I wanted to write a novel about a girl with the Caribbean in her blood, discovering her love of the Hudson Valley, as I did during the time I spent at Hawthorne Valley Farm. I deeply appreciate the welcome and community I was shown by everyone there, especially Safina Alessandra and Hilary Corsun. Thank you for the meals, hikes, crash pads, and, most of all, for answering my endless barrage of questions about farming, crafts, and conservation. Silver Meadows is an imaginary place, but I hope I have captured in these pages some of the wonder and love of the outdoors that you have imparted to me.

I'd also like to thank the brilliant editors who have worked with me on this manuscript. Harold Underdown's suggestions helped me determine the trajectory of this project, but much more importantly, I learned from Harold about the patience and dedication that go into revision. My agent, Adriana Dominguez, has been relentless in her support and always pushes me to do my best work. Her faith in her authors is evident in her high standards, and I treasure our conversations about Latinx families and literature.

I'd also like to thank Marisa DiNovis and Sylvia Al-Mateen for their detailed editorial feedback.

The first time I rode the subway with Jenny Brown, I knew she was my kind of person—someone with an encyclopedic knowledge of children's literature and a voracious reader. When my stop came, I didn't want to end our conversation about the past and future of children's books. I am incredibly grateful for this opportunity to continue the ride.

EMMA OTHEGUY is the author of the picture books *Martí's Song for Freedom,* which received five starred reviews, and, most recently, *Pope Francis: Builder of Bridges.* A resident of New York City, Emma is a member of the Bank Street Writers Lab and a historian of Spain and colonial Latin America. *Silver Meadows Summer* is her first middle-grade novel.

emmaotheguy.com